R. C R.

ms

good!
good!

LH very good!

Buffalo Valley

DEBBIE MACOMBER

Buffalo Valley

WHEELER
CHIVERS

This Large Print edition is published by Wheeler Publishing, Waterville, Maine USA and by BBC Audiobooks, Ltd, Bath, England.

Published in 2005 in the U.S. by arrangement with Harlequin Books S.A.

Published in 2005 in the U.K. by arrangement with Harlequin Enterprises II, B.V.

U.S. Hardcover 1-58724-877-8 (Romance)
U.K. Hardcover 1-4056-3254-2 (Chivers Large Print)
U.K. Softcover 1-4056-3255-0 (Camden Large Print)

The text of this Large Print edition is unabridged.
Other aspects of the book may vary from the original edition.

Set in 16 pt. Plantin by Ramona Watson.

Printed in the United States on permanent paper.

British Library Cataloguing-in-Publication Data available

Library of Congress Cataloging-in-Publication Data

Macomber, Debbie.
    Buffalo Valley / Debbie Macomber.
        p. cm.
    ISBN 1-58724-877-8 (lg. print : hc : alk. paper)
    1. North Dakota — Fiction.   2. Discount houses (Retail trade)
— Fiction.   3. Small business — Fiction.   4. Large type books.
I. Title.
PS3563.A2364B84 2005
    813'.54—dc22   2004043132

To
my mom and dad,
Ted and Connie Adler.
Boy, did I get lucky to have
you both for my parents!
I love you both.

Dear Friends,

I hope you enjoy this final journey to Buffalo Valley. As always, I found it difficult to set these characters and their community aside. Buffalo Valley will always remain a part of me because Dakota towns like this are part of my heritage.

Writing these four books has blessed me in a number of ways. Through my initial research trips, and later, when promoting the titles, I was privileged to meet some wonderful, down-home folks I'd consider it an honor to call friends. People like Erik Sakariassen and everyone at SAKS NEWS, and Matt Olien and the good people at Prairie Public Broadcasting station who generously gave me *Schmeckfest*, a video about the food traditions of Germans from Russia. We might not be able to correctly pronounce what we're eating, but it sure tastes good! The bookstores where I signed the trilogy books were terrific. MAXWELL'S BOOKS in Bismarck stayed open for me in the middle of a fierce windstorm; A NOVEL PLACE in Osseo, Minnesota, hosted one of the best signings I've ever done; the WALDENBOOKS in the Southridge Mall in Greendale, Wisconsin, attracted an enthusiastic crowd. Thank you, one and all.

A special bonus was becoming reacquainted with aunts, uncles and cousins. Aunt Gladys, you're a kick — and you're right, I haven't started decorating those eggs yet. Hey, my intentions are good! To Lettie and Gary, you promised to visit Wayne and me in Seattle and we're counting on it. To my cousin Paula and her husband, Mike — Wayne and I enjoyed the tour of your farm, including the directions on how to find you. (Was that the third dip in the road past the mile marker, or the second?)

To Aunt Betty and Uncle Vern, I love you both to death. I'm so blessed to have you in my life. Thank you for the incredible gift of laughter and example of your love. (My aunt Betty and uncle Vern have been married over seventy years, and when I mentioned how wonderful that was, my aunt said, "In all those years Vern has been tried and true." My uncle Vern, who's hard of hearing, replied with a snort, "Well, I'm tired of you, too!" See what I mean about the laughter?)

These books have been an adventure: the research, the writing, the touring and the good friends I've made along the way. I hope you'll enjoy one last trip to Buffalo Valley.

Warmest regards,
Debbie Macomber

The People of
Buffalo Valley, North Dakota
(introduced in the Dakota trilogy books)

Kevin Betts: Son of Leta and brother of Gage Sinclair

Leta Betts: Gage Sinclair's mother; Hassie Knight's good friend

Robert (Buffalo Bob) and Merrily Carr: Husband and wife who own 3 of a Kind (bar/restaurant/hotel)

John and Joyce Dawson: Local pastor and his wife

Margaret and Matt Eilers: Ranchers

Carrie Hendrickson: Works at Knight's Pharmacy as trainee pharmacist

Chuck and Ken Hendrickson: Carrie's unmarried brothers, still living at home and working at their father's hardware store.

Tom and Pete Hendrickson: Carrie's married brothers, who run the family ranch

Hassie Knight: Owner of Knight's Pharmacy. Unofficial town confidante and adviser. Has one daughter, Valerie, who lives in Hawaii with her two daughters

Jerry Knight: Hassie's deceased husband

Vaughn Knight: Hassie's son who died in Vietnam

Ambrose Kohn: Property owner planning to sell land to Value-X Corporation

Jeb and Maddy McKenna: Jeb ranches bison; Maddy owns the local grocery

Heath and Rachel Quantrill: Heath is president of Buffalo Valley Bank; Rachel owns and operates a pizza restaurant and burger stand

Lily Quantrill: Heath's grandmother, now deceased

Lindsay and Gage Sinclair: Lindsay teaches high school (now part-time); Gage is a farmer

Calla Stern: Sarah Urlacher's daughter. First-year law student in Chicago

Sarah and Dennis Urlacher: Sarah owns the Buffalo Valley Quilting Company; Dennis runs the local gas station

Joanie and Brandon Wyatt: Joanie owns a video rental and craft store in town; Brandon is a farmer

Chapter 1

So this was North Dakota. Gazing steadily ahead, Vaughn Kyle barreled down the freeway just outside Grand Forks. Within a few miles, the four lanes had narrowed to two. Dreary, dirt-smudged snow lay piled up along both sides of the highway. Fresh snow had begun to fall, pristine and bright, glinting in the late-afternoon sun.

His parents had retired earlier in the year, leaving Denver, where Vaughn had been born and raised, and returning to the state they'd left long ago. They'd moved north, away from the majestic peaks of the Rocky Mountains to the endlessly boring landscape of the Dakotas. *This* was supposed to be beautiful? Maybe in summer, he mused, when the fields of grain rippled with the wind, acre after acre. Now, though, in December, in the dead of winter, the beauty of this place escaped him. All that was visible was a winding stretch of black asphalt cutting through flat, monotonous terrain that stretched for miles in every direction.

After seven years as an Airborne Ranger in the U.S. Army's Second Battalion based in

Fort Lewis, Washington, Vaughn was poised to begin the second stage of his working life. He had his discharge papers and he'd recently been hired by Value-X, a mega-retailer with headquarters in Seattle. Value-X was one of America's most notable success stories. New stores were opening every day all across the United States and Canada.

His course was set for the future, thanks largely to Natalie Nichols. They'd met two years earlier through mutual friends. Natalie was smart, savvy and ambitious; Value-X had recognized her skills and she'd advanced quickly, being promoted to a vice presidency before the age of thirty.

Vaughn had been attracted by her dedication and purpose, and he'd admired her ambition. His own work ethic was strong; as he'd come to realize, that was increasingly rare in this age of quick fixes and no-fault living. Natalie was the one who'd convinced him to leave the army. He was ready. When he'd enlisted after finishing college, he'd done so intending to make the military his career. In the seven years since, he'd learned the advantages and drawbacks of soldiering.

He didn't mind the regimented life, but the career possibilities weren't all he'd hoped they would be. What he lacked, as Natalie had pointed out, was opportunity. He was limited in how far he could rise through the ranks or how quickly, while the private sector was wide-open and looking for promising employees like him. He'd been interviewed by three headhunters who recruited candidates for a variety of corporations and in just a few weeks had six job offers.

At first he'd felt there might be a conflict of interest, taking a position with the same company as Natalie. However, she didn't view it that way; they would be a team, she'd told Vaughn, and with that remarkable persuasive skill of hers had convinced him to come on board. He wouldn't officially start until after the first of the year, but he was already on assignment.

Value-X was buying property in Buffalo Valley, North Dakota. Since Vaughn was going to be in the vicinity, visiting his parents in nearby Grand Forks, Natalie had asked him to pay the town a visit. It wasn't uncommon for a community to put up token resistance to the company's arrival. In most cases, any negative publicity was successfully handled, using a proven strategy that included barraging the local media with stories showing the company's "human face." After a recent public-relations disaster in Montana, Natalie was eager to avoid a repeat. She'd asked Vaughn to do a "climate check" in Buffalo Valley, but it was important, she insisted, that he not let anyone know he was now a Value-X employee, not even his parents. Vaughn had reluctantly agreed.

He'd done this because he trusted Natalie's judgment. And because he was in love with her. They'd talked about marriage, although she seemed hesitant. Her reasons for postponing it were logical, presented in her usual no-nonsense manner. She refused to be "subservient to emotion," as she called it, and Vaughn was impressed by her clear-cut vision of what she wanted and how to achieve it. They'd get married when the time was right for both of them.

He was eager to have her meet his family. Natalie would be joining him on December twenty-seventh, but he wished she could've rearranged her schedule to travel with him.

On this cold Friday afternoon two weeks before Christmas, Vaughn had decided to drive into Buffalo Valley. Because of Hassie Knight, he didn't need to invent an excuse for his parents. Hassie was the mother of his namesake. She'd lost her only son — his parents' closest friend — in Vietnam three years before Vaughn was born. Every birthday, until he'd reached the age of twenty-one, Hassie had mailed him a letter with a twenty-five-dollar U.S. Savings Bond.

In all that time, he'd never met her. From first grade on, he'd dutifully sent her a thank-you note for every gift. That was the extent of their contact, but he still felt a genuine fondness for her — and gratitude. Hassie had been the one to start him on a savings program. As a young adult Vaughn had cashed in those savings bonds and begun acquiring a portfolio of stocks that over the years had become a hefty nest egg.

An hour after he left Grand Forks, Vaughn slowed his speed, certain that if he blinked he might miss Buffalo Valley entirely. Value-X could put this place on the map. That was one benefit the company offered small towns. He wasn't sure what kind of business community existed in Buffalo Valley. He knew about Knight's Pharmacy of course, because Hassie owned that. Apparently the town was large enough to have its own cemetery, too; Hassie had mailed him a picture of her son's gravesite years earlier.

Buffalo Valley was directly off the road. You didn't take an exit the way you would in most places. You just drove off the highway. He slowed, made a right turn where the road sign indicated. The car pitched as it left the pavement and hit ruts in the frozen dirt road. He'd gone at least a hundred feet before the paved road resumed.

He passed a few scattered houses, and as he turned the corner, he discovered, somewhat to his surprise, a main street with businesses lining both sides. There was even a hotel of sorts, called Buffalo Bob's 3 of a Kind. The bank building, a sprawling brick structure, seemed new and quite extensive. This was amazing. He wasn't sure what he'd

15

expected, but nothing like this. Buffalo Valley was a real town, not a cluster of run-down houses and boarded-up stores, like some of the prairie towns his parents had told him about.

Hassie's store caught his attention next. It was a quaint, old-fashioned pharmacy, with big picture windows and large white lettering. Christmas lights framed the window, flashing alternately red and green. In smaller letters below KNIGHT'S PHARMACY, a soda fountain was advertised. Vaughn hadn't tasted a real soda made with hand-scooped ice cream and flavored syrup since his childhood.

He parked, climbed out of his rental car and stood on the sidewalk, glancing around. This was a decent-size town, decorated for the holidays with festive displays in nearly every window. A city park could be seen in the distance, and the Buffalo Valley Quilting Company appeared to take up a large portion of the block across the street. He remembered an article about it in the file Natalie had given him.

The cold stung his face and snow swirled around him. Rather than stand there risking frostbite, Vaughn walked into the pharmacy. The bell above the door jingled and he was instantly greeted by a blast of heat that chased the chill from his bones.

"Can I help you?" He couldn't see who spoke, but the voice sounded young, so he assumed it wasn't Hassie. The woman or girl, whoever she was, stood behind the raised counter at the back of the store.

"I'm looking for Hassie Knight," Vaughn called, edging his way down the narrow aisle. This pharmacy apparently carried everything: cosmetics, greeting cards, over-the-counter medicine, gourmet chocolate, toothpaste and tissues — just about anything you might require.

"I'm sorry, Hassie's out for the day. Can I be of help?"

He supposed he didn't need to see Hassie, although it would have been nice.

"I'm Carrie Hendrickson." A petite blonde in a white jacket materialized before him, hand extended. "I'm an intern working with Hassie."

"Vaughn Kyle," he said, stretching out his own hand. He liked the way her eyes squarely met his. Her expression held a hint of suspicion, but Vaughn was prepared for that. Natalie had mentioned the North Dakota attitude toward strangers — a wariness that ranged from mild doubt to outright hostility. It was one reason she worried about this proposed building site.

"Hassie and I have never officially met, but she does know me," he added reassuringly. "I was named after her son."

"You're *the* Vaughn Kyle?" she asked, her voice revealing excitement now. "Did Hassie

17

know you were coming and completely forget? I can't imagine her doing that."

"No, no, it was nothing like that. I just happened to be in the area and thought I'd stop by and introduce myself."

Her suspicion evaporated and was replaced with a wide, welcoming smile. "I'm so pleased to meet you. Hassie will be thrilled." She gestured to the counter. "Can I get you anything? Coffee? A soft drink?"

"Actually, I wouldn't mind an old-fashioned soda."

"They're Hassie's specialty, but I'll do my best."

"Don't worry about it." On second thought, he decided something warm might be preferable. "I'll have a coffee."

She led him to the soda fountain and Vaughn sat on a padded stool while Carrie ducked beneath the counter and reappeared on the other side.

"Do you know when Hassie's due back?" he asked.

"Around six," Carrie told him, lifting the glass pot and filling his cup. "You need space for cream?" she asked.

He answered with a quick shake of his head. She didn't cut off the steady stream of weak coffee until it'd reached the very brim of his cup.

The door opened, bells jingling, and a woman dressed in a black leather jacket

18

walked into the store. She had three scarves wrapped around her neck, nearly obscuring her face.

"Hi, Merrily," Carrie called, then scrambled under the fountain barrier. "I'll have Bobby's prescription ready in just a moment." She hurried to the back of the store. "While you're waiting, introduce yourself to Vaughn Kyle."

Merrily glanced toward the counter and waved, and Vaughn raised his mug to her.

"That's *Hassie's* Vaughn Kyle," Carrie said emphatically. "Vaughn was named after her son," she added.

"Well, why didn't you say so?" Merrily walked over to shake his hand. "What are you doing here?" she asked, unwinding the woolen scarves.

Now, that was an interesting question, Vaughn thought. He certainly hadn't anticipated anyone knowing about him.

"He came to meet Hassie," Carrie said as she returned with the prescription. She handed Merrily a small white sack. "How's Bobby feeling?"

"Better, I think. Poor little guy seems prone to ear infections." She turned to Vaughn with a smile. "Nice meeting you," she said. She wrapped the mufflers around her face again before she headed out the door.

"You, too," Vaughn murmured.

Carrie reached across the counter and grabbed a second mug for herself. "Hassie told you about the War Memorial, didn't she? We're all proud of that." Not waiting for a response, she continued, "The town built the Memorial three years ago, and it honors everyone from Buffalo Valley who died in war. The only one most of us actually remember is Hassie's son. But there were others. We lost Harvey Schmidt in the Korean War and five men in World War II, but none of their families live in the area anymore."

"You knew Vaughn Knight?" The blonde seemed far too young to have known Hassie's son.

"Not personally. But from the time I was small, Hassie told my brothers and me about Vaughn. It's been her mission to make sure he isn't forgotten."

Vaughn had heard about Vaughn Knight from his own parents of course, since they'd both been close to Hassie's son.

Carrie sipped her coffee. "Hassie told me it was one of the greatest honors of her life that your parents chose to remember her son through you."

Vaughn nodded, disappointed that he'd missed meeting the older woman. "What time did you say Hassie would be back?"

"Around six, I guess."

Vaughn checked his watch. He didn't intend to make an entire day of this.

"If Hassie had known you were coming, I don't think *anything* could've kept her away."

"I should have phoned beforehand," he muttered. "But . . ."

"I hope you'll wait."

Vaughn glanced at his watch again. Three hours was far longer than he wanted to stick around. "Tell her I'll come by some other time."

"*Please* stay. Hassie would feel terrible if she learned you'd left without meeting her." She hesitated, obviously thinking. "Listen," she said, "I'll phone Leta Betts and ask if she can fill in for me for a couple of hours."

Vaughn reconsidered. He might get all the information he needed from Carrie; then he could meet Hassie on strictly social terms. He'd been vaguely uncomfortable about questioning Hassie, anyway.

"Please," she said, "it would mean the world to Hassie, and I'd be delighted to give you a tour of town."

Perfect. He'd learn everything Natalie wanted to know and more. "That's a generous offer. Are you sure you don't mind?"

"I'd consider it a pleasure," she said, and smiled.

With her looking up at him that way, smiling and appreciative, Vaughn couldn't help noticing that Carrie Hendrickson was a very attractive woman. Not that Natalie had anything to worry about, he told himself staunchly.

Working closely with Hassie as an intern pharmacist, Carrie Hendrickson was keenly aware of how eager the older woman was to meet her son's namesake. A few months ago, Hassie had heard that the Kyles had retired in Grand Forks and she'd mailed off a note, inviting them to visit Buffalo Valley. Apparently they planned to do that sometime in the new year. Hassie would be ecstatic about finally meeting their son.

Carrie loved Hassie Knight, who was her mentor and her friend. Following Carrie's divorce, Hassie had given her sympathy — and good, brisk, commonsense advice. She'd guided her through the fog of her pain and encouraged her to look toward the future. Many an afternoon they'd spent talking, reminiscing, sitting quietly together. Hassie had shared the grief of her own losses and helped Carrie deal with Alec's betrayal in ways her own mother never could. Hassie was the person who'd suggested she return to college. Carrie had taken her advice; nearly six years ago she'd enrolled at the University of North Dakota in Grand Forks. Now she was about to finish her internship with Knight's Pharmacy and achieve her Pharm.D and become a Doctor of Pharmacy. The last few years had been bleak financially, but the reward would be worth all the sacrifices.

After her divorce, she'd moved back in with her parents. She felt deeply grateful for their generosity but she *was* twenty-seven years old and longed for more independence and a home of her own. Well, it would happen eventually; she'd just have to wait.

Meanwhile, working side by side with Hassie, Carrie had learned a great deal. When it came time for the older woman to retire, Carrie would be willing and able to assume her role in the pharmacy and in the town. People knew and trusted her. Already they approached her with their troubles and concerns as naturally as they did Hassie. Alec's infidelity had reinforced the importance of trust and honor for Carrie. Those were precepts she lived by. The people of Buffalo Valley knew she would keep their problems to herself.

The town was a success story in an area where there'd been few. The Hendrickson farm, like many others, had fallen victim to low crop prices. Unable to make a living farming the land that had supported them for three generations, her father had leased the acreage to his older sons and moved into town. Together with Carrie's two younger brothers, he'd opened a hardware store.

For as long as she could remember, Knight's Pharmacy had been the very heart of this town. Hassie was getting on in years and probably should've retired long ago. She wouldn't, though, not while the community still needed her, not only to dispense prescriptions and basic medical advice but also to be their counselor and confidante.

Carrie knew she could never replace Hassie, because that would be impossible. But she'd always been good at chemistry and math, and had done well at her pharmaceutical studies. She also cared about the town and had an intense interest in people. Hassie had often told her she was naturally intuitive and sensitive toward others; Carrie was pleased by that, although her intuition had been notably absent during her ex-husband's affair. Hassie said she was exactly the pharmacist Buffalo Valley needed and had given her the faith in herself to believe she could complete the six years of schooling required to obtain her license.

"I'll get my coat and hat and be right back," she told Vaughn after calling Leta. Hassie's friend worked at the pharmacy part-time and was as eager as Carrie to make sure that Hassie met Vaughn.

"You're certain this isn't an imposition?"

"Absolutely certain," she told him.

Leta arrived promptly and after making swift introductions, Carrie removed the white pharmacist's jacket and put on her long wool coat.

"What would you like to see first?" she asked when she rejoined him.

"Whatever you'd like to show me."

"Then let's go to the City Park." Although there were a number of places she wanted to take him, the park seemed the best place to start. As they left the pharmacy, Carrie noticed it had stopped snowing, but she suspected the temperature had dropped several degrees. She led him across the street and then down a block, past the quilt store and several others.

"I know Hassie would want you to see the War Memorial," she said, glancing up at Vaughn. Now that she stood beside him, she was surprised to see how tall he was — possibly six-two. All four of her brothers were six feet, but Carrie took after her mother's side of the family and was small-boned and petite. His dark good looks didn't escape her notice, either.

"First came the park," she explained, walking briskly to ward off the cold. Carrie loved the City Park and everything it said about their community. The people of Buffalo Valley had worked together to make this barren plot of land a place of which to be proud. "The land itself was a gift from Lily Quantrill," she said. "Heath Quantrill, her grandson, is the president of Buffalo Valley Bank." She pointed toward the brick structure at the far end of Main Street.

"Isn't there a branch in Grand Forks?"

"There are branches all across the state," Carrie told him.

"The headquarters is here?"

She nodded. "Heath moved everything to Buffalo Valley two years ago. I know it was a hard decision, but this is his home now, and he was tired of commuting to Grand Forks three days a week."

"It's an impressive building."

"Heath's an impressive bank president. I hope you get the chance to meet him and his wife, Rachel."

"I do, too," Vaughn said.

"Heath donated the lumber for the children's play equipment," she said as they entered the park and strolled past the jungle gym, slides and swings. "But Brandon Wyatt, along with Jeb McKenna and Gage Sinclair, actually built all these things." She realized the names didn't mean anything to Vaughn, but she wanted him to get a sense of what the park stood for in this community. Each family had contributed something, from planting the grass to laying the concrete walkway.

"It looks well used."

An outsider like Vaughn couldn't possibly understand how much the children of Buffalo Valley cherished the park. "My family owns the hardware," she continued, pointing to the opposite side of the park toward the store. "We donated the wood for the picnic tables."

"I notice they aren't secured with chains," Vaughn said.

"We don't have much crime in Buffalo Valley." It distressed her to visit public areas where everything, including picnic tables and garbage cans, was tied down by chains to prevent theft. But no one had ever stolen from the park or any other public place in Buffalo Valley. There'd never been any real vandalism, either.

"No crime?" He sounded as though he didn't believe her.

"Well, some, but it's mostly petty stuff. A few windows soaped at Halloween, that kind of thing. The occasional fight or display of drunkenness. We did have a murder once, about eighty years ago. According to the stories, it was a crime of passion." Quickly changing the subject, she said, "The War Memorial was designed by Kevin Betts. I don't know if you've heard of him, but he was born and raised right here."

"Sorry, I haven't," Vaughn said with a shrug.

"He's Leta's son, and he's an artist who's making a name for himself." Everyone in town was proud of Kevin. "This sculpture —" she gestured as they neared it "— was one of his very first." She watched Vaughn's expression when he saw it and was stirred by the immediate appreciation that showed in his eyes.

Kevin was a gifted artist, not only because he was technically skilled but because his

27

work evoked emotion in people. The bronze sculpture was simple and yet profound. Half-a-dozen rifles were stacked together, upright and leaning against one another, with a helmet balanced on top. Beside the guns a young soldier knelt, his shoulders bowed in grief. No one seeing the piece could fail to be moved, to respond with sorrow and a bittersweet pain.

Vaughn stood before the memorial and didn't say anything right away. Then he squatted down and ran his finger over the name of Vaughn Knight. "My parents still talk about him. He was the one who brought them together," Vaughn said, and slowly straightened. "I'm glad he won't be forgotten."

"He won't be," Carrie assured him. "With this memorial, his name will always be here to remind everyone."

Vaughn thrust his gloved hands into his coat pockets.

"Cold?" Carrie asked.

He shook his head. "I know about the pharmacy and you've mentioned the hardware store. Tell me about the other businesses in town."

They walked toward Main Street and Carrie told him about each one in turn, starting with Joanie Wyatt's video-rental and craft store and ending with her parents' place.

"It was a leap of faith for you to move into town, wasn't it?" Vaughn said.

Carrie nodded pensively. "Yeah, but it's paid off. My two oldest brothers are still farming and the two younger ones work exclusively with Mom and Dad. It's a good arrangement all around."

"Are you hungry?" Vaughn asked unexpectedly.

She laughed. "You offering to feed me?" It was a bit early, but dinner would pass the time until Hassie returned.

"Unless there's a reason for you to hurry home."

"No reason. I'm divorced." Even now, six years later, the words left a bitter taste on her tongue. She focused her gaze directly in front of her.

"I'm sorry," he said.

"I am, too." She forced a cheerful note into her voice, as if to say she was over it.

"I thought I'd suggest Buffalo Bob's 3 of a Kind. I was intrigued by what you told me about him."

"He's certainly a character," she agreed. "But before we go there, I'd like to show you Maddy's Grocery." Carrie loved the wonderful and witty Christmas display Maddy put up every year. Eight reindeer were suspended from the ceiling, with the front half of Santa's sleigh coming out of the wall.

Vaughn laughed when he saw it. His reaction

was one of genuine enjoyment and not the short derisive laugh of someone mocking Maddy's efforts. On their way to 3 of a Kind, they strolled past the Buffalo Valley Quilting Company.

"This is the success story of the decade," Carrie boasted as she motioned to the holiday quilt displayed in the first set of windows. "Sarah Urlacher started the business in her father's house, dyeing the muslin herself from all-natural products. The designs are her own, too."

Vaughn stopped to look at the quilt in the window.

"It all began when Lindsay Sinclair introduced Sarah's quilts to her uncle. He owns an upscale furniture store in Atlanta, and before she knew it, Sarah had trouble keeping up with the demand. Now people all over the country buy her quilts."

"That's great."

"Sarah's business has boosted the economy of Buffalo Valley to the point that we can now afford things that are commonplace in other towns."

"Such as?"

"The sidewalks got refurbished last summer, and the town could never have paid for that without the tax revenue Sarah's business brings in." Carrie didn't mention the new community well and several other improvements that had taken place over the past few years.

"I'll let Leta know where we are so she can tell Hassie," Carrie said, and made a quick stop at the pharmacy. She was back within moments. Vaughn waited for her outside.

There was no one at the restaurant or in the bar when they arrived. Studying Buffalo Bob with fresh eyes, Carrie could only guess what Vaughn must think. The ex-biker was a burly man. He was an oddity here in a town where most men came off the farm. With his thinning hair drawn back into a ponytail and his muscular arms covered in tattoos, he looked as though he'd be more comfortable with a biker gang than waiting tables.

"How ya doin', Carrie?" he greeted her when she took a seat across the table from Vaughn.

"Good, Bob. Come meet Vaughn Kyle."

"Welcome to Buffalo Valley," Bob said, extending his hand for a hearty shake. "Merrily told me you'd dropped by." Bob gave them each a menu. "Take a look, but the special tonight is Salisbury steak. I don't mind telling you it's excellent." He grinned. "And who would know better than me?"

"I'm convinced," Vaughn told him with an answering smile. "I'll have the special."

"Me, too," Carrie said, returning the menu.

Bob left them, and Carrie tried to relax but found it difficult. She hadn't been alone with a man, other than her brothers, in a very long time. Following her divorce, she'd

31

only dated twice, and both occasions had been awkward. Her schooling, plus her internship, didn't leave much room for a social life, anyway.

Vaughn sat back in his chair. "Tell me about Hassie," he suggested easily.

Carrie felt the tightness leave her shoulders. On the subject of Hassie, she could talk his ear off. "What would you like to know first?"

"Whatever you feel is important."

"She's been my hero for as long as I can remember. I don't know what would've happened to this town without her." Carrie wanted him to realize how deeply Hassie was loved by everyone in Buffalo Valley. "She's older now, and she's slowing down some." Carrie had seen the evidence of that in the months since she'd come to work as an intern. She almost suspected that Hassie had been holding on until she got there.

Vaughn glanced at Buffalo Bob as he brought their salads and nodded his thanks. "Every year, along with my birthday card and a U.S. Savings Bond, she wrote me a short message." His mouth lifted in a half smile. "She called it *words to live by.*"

"Give me an example," Carrie said, curious.

"I don't remember them all, but . . . okay, she told me about the importance of being on time. Only, she did it by making up this little poem. . . ." He hesitated and a slow grin crossed his face. "She once wrote that if at first I don't succeed, it just means I'm normal."

"That sounds like Hassie."

"She has a wonderful way of putting things." He paused, a reflective look on his face. "When I was sixteen, she told me the grass isn't greener on the other side of the fence, it's greener where it's watered."

"I think it's wonderful that you remembered them."

"How could I not, when she made them so much fun? She was like an extra grandmother."

Hearing that warmed Carrie's heart, because she knew Hassie felt toward him the way she would a grandson.

They were silent as they ate their salads. Buffalo Bob had made even a plain lettuce, cucumber and tomato salad taste delicious with the addition of a tart-sweet cranberry dressing. They were just finishing when Bob reappeared, carrying two plates heaped with food. He placed them in front of Vaughn and Carrie, then stepped back, and said, "Enjoy."

Vaughn stared after him as he returned to the kitchen. "He's not the typical sort of person you find in a place like this, is he?"

"Bob's a sweetheart," she said defensively. "He's hardworking and well-liked and a wonderful father and —"

"Tell me how he happened to land in

Buffalo Valley," Vaughn broke in. He reached for his fork, tasting the fluffy mashed potatoes and tender gravy-covered steak.

"He came here when the town was at its lowest point. My uncle Earl owned this hotel and he'd been trying to sell it for years. Seeing that there weren't any buyers and he was losing money every month, my uncle devised an unusual poker game. It cost a thousand dollars to play, but the winner walked away with the hotel, restaurant and bar. Lock, stock and barrel."

Vaughn's brows arched. "And Bob won it with three of a kind."

"Exactly."

Vaughn shook his head. "More power to him."

"A lot has changed since then, all of it for the better. Bob married Merrily, and two and a half years ago, they had little Bobby."

"The one who's prone to ear infections?"

She nodded. "You've never seen better parents. Those two dote on that little boy something fierce. In fact, Bob and Merrily are terrific with all the kids in town." Carrie paused long enough to sample her dinner. "Hey, this is terrific."

Vaughn agreed with her. "In addition to his other talents, Buffalo Bob's a good cook. He wasn't kidding about that."

"I don't know what his life was like before

34

he came to Buffalo Valley, but he's one of us now."

Vaughn was about to ask a question when the door opened and Hassie hurried inside.

Carrie was instantly on her feet. One look told her Hassie was exhausted. Her shoulders were slumped and she seemed close to collapse.

"Hassie," Carrie said, wrapping her arm protectively around the older woman's waist. "This is Vaughn Kyle."

It was almost as if Hassie didn't hear her at first. "Vaughn," she repeated, and then her face brightened visibly. "My goodness, did you let me know you were coming and it slipped my mind?"

Vaughn pulled out a chair for her to sit down. "No, I very rudely showed up without an invitation."

"I wish I'd known."

"It's no problem. Carrie was kind enough to spend the afternoon with me."

"Let me take a good look at you," Hassie said. She cupped his face with both hands and a smile emerged. "You're so handsome," she whispered. "You have such kind eyes."

If her praise embarrassed or flustered him, Vaughn didn't reveal it.

"How long can you stay?" she asked.

"Actually, I should probably think about heading back to Grand Forks soon."

"No," Hassie protested. "That's hardly

enough time for me to show you everything."

"Carrie already gave me a tour of town."

"That's good, but I have a number of things I've saved that I'd like you to have — things that were my son's."

Her disappointment was unmistakeable, and Carrie glanced at Vaughn, trying to signal him, hoping he'd change his mind.

"I want to see them."

Carrie could have hugged him right then and there.

"But," he added, "you've had a long, tiring day. Perhaps it would be better if I came back later."

Hassie didn't bother to deny what was obvious. "Would it be too much to ask you to come here on Sunday?" Both her hands gripped his, as if she was afraid to let him go.

Carrie found herself just as eager to hear his response.

"I'll meet you at the store shortly after noon," he said. "I'll look forward to seeing you then."

Carrie felt a surge of relief — and anticipation. She couldn't help smiling, first at Hassie, then at Vaughn.

Happiness shimmered in the old woman's eyes as she placed one hand on Carrie's shoulder and leaned heavily against her.

"That would be perfect," she said quietly. "Thank you, Vaughn."

Chapter 2

Hassie felt old and weary, especially after a day like this. But God had rewarded her patience by sending Vaughn Kyle to Buffalo Valley. Seeing him, however briefly, had lifted her spirits. Best of all was his promise to return on Sunday afternoon.

Tired though she was, Hassie brewed herself a cup of tea and sat at her kitchen table, mulling over the events of the day. Ambrose Kohn had been a thorn in her side for many years. His family had lived and worked in town for generations, but with impeccable timing, the Kohns had moved to Devils Lake just before the economy in Buffalo Valley collapsed.

Ambrose owned several pieces of property here and a building or two. The theater belonged to him, and he'd been quick enough to close it down, despite the town council's efforts to convince him otherwise. The old building still had plenty of life in it, but it'd sat abandoned and neglected until the first year Lindsay Snyder came to Buffalo Valley as the high-school teacher. She'd wanted to use it for a Christmas play. If Hassie remembered correctly, Ambrose had demanded she go out with him first before he gave permission. That annoyed Hassie even now, several years later.

Lindsay had attended some social function with Ambrose, and it had nearly ruined her relationship with Gage Sinclair. But she and Gage had resolved their differences. They'd been married for more than five years now and were parents of two beautiful daughters.

Ambrose, despite his underhanded methods, had walked away a winner, as well. After the community had cleaned up that old theater and put on the high-school Christmas program, he'd reopened the movie house and it'd been in operation ever since.

Unfortunately Ambrose hadn't learned anything from that experience. He hadn't learned that people in Buffalo Valley loved their town and that they supported one another. He hadn't figured out that for them, Buffalo Valley was *home,* not just a place to live. Now the middle-aged bachelor held the fate of the community in his hands. Value-X, a huge retailer, wanted to move into town and they wanted to set up shop on land owned by Ambrose. The company had a reputation for sweeping into small towns and then systematically destroying independent and family-owned businesses. Six months earlier, Hassie had watched a television report on the effect the mega-retailer had on communities.

At the time she'd never dreamed Buffalo Valley might be targeted. Naturally the company insisted this was progress and a boon to the town's economy. There were already articles in some of the regional papers, touting the company's supposedly civic-minded attitudes. Profit-minded was more like it.

No one needed to tell Hassie what would happen to Buffalo Valley if Value-X decided to follow through with its plans. All the small businesses that had recently started would die a fast and painful death. Her own pharmacy wouldn't be immune.

Ambrose owned twenty acres just outside of town; this was the property Value-X was interested in acquiring, and he wasn't opposed to selling it — no matter how badly it damaged the community.

Nothing Hassie said had the least bit of impact on him. Buffalo Bob, as president of the town council, had tried to reason with him, too, again without success. Heath Quantrill had thrown up his hands in frustration at the man's stubborn refusal to listen.

While Ambrose didn't live in Buffalo Valley, he did have a powerful influence on its future. For that reason alone, he should think carefully about his decision to sell that parcel of land. Progress or not, it wasn't the kind of future she or anyone here saw for Buffalo Valley. Jerry, her husband, might have been able to talk sense into Ambrose, but

Jerry had died the year after Vaughn. She'd lost them both so close together.

The TV report on Value-X had made a strong impression on Hassie. What had stayed in her mind most clearly were the interviews with business owners, some with three- and four-generation histories. They'd been forced to close down, unable to compete. Local traditions had been lost, pride broken. Men and women wept openly, in despair and hopelessness. Downtown areas died out.

Hassie couldn't bear to think what would happen to Buffalo Valley if Ambrose sold that land to those outsiders. Why, it would undo all the work the town council had done over the past six years. The outcome was too dismal to consider.

Joanie Wyatt's video-rental and craft store would probably be one of the first to fold. And the Hendricksons — they'd sunk everything they had in this world and more into AceMan Hardware. Value-X would undercut the lowest prices they could charge and ring the store's death knell for sure.

Dennis Urlacher supplied car parts to the community at his filling station. Although that was only a small portion of his business, Dennis had once mentioned that his largest profit margin came from the auto parts and not the fuel. It wouldn't be long before his business was affected, too. Even Rachel

Quantrill's new hamburger stand would lose customers. Maddy's Grocery would suffer, too; how long she'd be able to hold on depended on Value-X's plans. It was said that many of the newer stores included groceries.

None of that concerned Ambrose. All he knew was that he'd been offered a fair price for a piece of land that had sat vacant for years. He'd let it be known that he fully intended to sell those acres. If anyone else was interested, he'd entertain other offers. Ambrose had made one thing perfectly clear: the offer had to be substantially higher than the deal Value-X had proposed. No one in town, not even Heath Quantrill, had a thick-enough bankroll to get into a bidding war with the huge retailer.

Hassie sipped her tea and purposely turned her thoughts in a more pleasant direction. What a fine-looking young man Vaughn Kyle was. After all these years, she was grateful to finally meet him. His letters had meant so much to her, and she'd saved each thank-you note from the time he was six years old.

For a short while after her son was buried, Hassie and Barbara, the boy's mother, had been close. They'd stayed in touch, but then a year later the wedding announcement arrived. Barbara, the beautiful young woman her son had loved, was marrying Rick Kyle, who'd been one of Vaughn's best friends.

Hassie didn't begrudge the couple happiness,

but she hadn't attended the wedding. Their marriage was a painful reminder that life continues. If circumstances had been different, this might have been her own son's wedding.

Two years later, Rick and Barbara had mailed her the birth announcement. They'd named their first child after Hassie's son. Two years later came another birth announcement, this time for a girl they named Gloria. Sight unseen, Hassie had loved that boy and thought of him as the grandson Vaughn could never give her. Her own daughter, Valerie, had two girls and Hassie adored them, but since Val and her family lived in Hawaii, there was little opportunity to see them. Vaughn Kyle had assumed a special significance for her. Neither his parents nor anyone else knew how deep her feelings ran. With a determined effort, she'd remained on the sidelines of his life, writing occasional letters and sending gifts at the appropriate times.

Now she would have the opportunity to give Vaughn the things she'd set aside for him so many years ago. It'd been her prayer that they meet before she died.

She had to stop herself from being greedy. She would gladly accept whatever time Vaughn Kyle was willing to grant her.

Carrie found herself smiling as she walked into the family home shortly after six. She paused in the entryway to remove the handknit scarf from around her neck and shrug out of her coat. Softly humming a Christmas tune, she savored the warm feelings left by her visit with Vaughn. She'd enjoyed getting to know him. Even though it'd been years since she'd spent this much time in a man's company, the initial awkwardness between them had dissipated quickly.

Vaughn seemed genuinely interested in learning what he could about Hassie and Buffalo Valley. What she appreciated most was that he hadn't asked any prying questions about her divorce. A lot of people assumed she wanted to tell her side of it, but Carrie found no joy in reliving the most painful, humiliating experience of her life.

Their dinner conversation had flowed smoothly. He was easy to talk to, and Carrie loved telling him about Buffalo Valley. She was proud to recount its history, especially the developments of the past five years. The improvements could be attributed to several factors, but almost all of them went right back to Hassie Knight and her determination and optimism. Hassie refused to let the town fade into nothingness, refused to let it die like countless other communities throughout the Dakotas.

When Carrie walked into the living room, her mother glanced up from her needlework and her two younger brothers hurried in from the kitchen. All three fixed their eyes on her. Everyone seemed to be waiting for her to speak.

"*What?*" Carrie demanded.

"We're curious about your dinner date," her mother said mildly.

Carrie should've realized her family would hear she'd gone out with Vaughn. *How* they knew she could only speculate, but in a small town word traveled even faster than it did on the Internet.

"How'd it go?" Ken asked, looking as though he'd welcome the opportunity to defend her honor should the occasion arise.

Part of the pain of her divorce came from knowing that she was the first in their family's history to whom it had happened. Longstanding marriages were a tradition she would gladly have continued. But she couldn't stay married to a man who didn't honor his vows, a man whose unfaithfulness undermined her self-respect, as well as their marriage. Her four brothers had hinted that things with Alec would have worked out differently if they'd been around to see to it. Needless to say, the last thing she wanted was her brothers, much as she loved them, playing the role of enforcers.

"He's very nice," she said, carefully weighing her words. She didn't want to give the impression that there was more to their meeting than a simple, friendly dinner.

"He didn't try anything, did he?" Chuck asked.

Carrie nearly laughed out loud. "Of course he didn't. Where's Dad?" she asked, wondering why her father hadn't leaped into the conversation.

Before anyone could respond, her father shuffled into the room, wearing his old slippers, a newspaper tucked under his arm and his reading glasses perched on the end of his nose. He stopped abruptly when he saw her.

"So how was your hot date?" he asked. He stood in front of his easy chair and waited for her to answer.

"It was just dinner," she protested. "The only reason he asked me out was to kill time while he waited for Hassie." It was unlikely they'd be doing this again, which she supposed was just as well. She had to admit she *wanted* to, but from what he'd said, he was only in the area for the Christmas holidays and then he was going home to Seattle. There was no point in starting something you couldn't finish, she thought. Not that she knew if he was even interested in her . . . or available.

"Will you be seeing him again?" her mother asked, but Carrie wasn't fooled by her nonchalant tone.

"He's coming back Sunday afternoon to —"

"That's great." Her mother smiled, clearly pleased.

"He isn't returning to see *me*." It was important her family understand that she had nothing to do with his decision. The sole reason for his visit was to spend time with Hassie.

"That's a shame." Her father claimed his chair, turning automatically to the sports page.

"Did you invite him to the tree-lighting ceremony?" Ken asked.

Her father lowered the newspaper and her mother paused in the middle of a stitch to await her response.

"No," Carrie admitted reluctantly. She'd thought of mentioning it, but couldn't see the purpose. She glanced around the room, looking at each hopeful face.

What she didn't say was that she would've welcomed the opportunity to know Vaughn Kyle better. The few hours she'd spent with him had helped her realize that her heart was still capable of response, that it hadn't shriveled up inside her like an orange left too long in the fruit bowl.

For that she was grateful.

As Vaughn pulled the rental car into the long driveway that led to his parents' home, he saw that his mother had turned on the back porch light. It wasn't really necessary, since the outside of the entire house was decorated with Christmas lights.

He knew his mother had made tentative plans for a dinner with friends on Sunday afternoon and might not be pleased by his absence. However, Vaughn didn't mind returning to Buffalo Valley. He'd enjoyed meeting Carrie and learning some of the town's recent history. He'd report this information to Natalie; she might find it useful. Carrie Hendrickson was an interesting contrast to the women he'd met and dated in Seattle during the past few years — including Natalie, his sort-of fiancée. Carrie had shied away from talking about herself, which was a refreshing change from what he'd grown accustomed to hearing. A recent dinner date with Natalie had been spent discussing every aspect of her career and the Value-X corporation — as if their work was all they had to talk about. He'd come away with a letdown feeling, feeling, somehow, that he'd missed out on something important . . . only he didn't know quite what. After all, he *admired* Natalie's drive and ambition and her unemotional approach to life.

His mother was finishing the dinner dishes when he entered the kitchen. "How was your visit?" she asked, rinsing a pan before setting it on the drainboard.

"Wonderful."

"How's Hassie?" she asked, looking expectantly at him as she reached for the towel to dry her hands. "You did give her my love, didn't you?"

"She was exhausted." He explained that the

pharmacist had been at a meeting when he arrived and that her assistant had convinced him to wait until she got back. Neither she nor Carrie had mentioned the reason for the meeting, but whatever it was had drained her, emotionally and physically.

His mother's brow furrowed with concern. "She's not ill, is she?"

"I don't think so, but I didn't want to tire her out any more than she already was, so I told her I'd be back on Sunday."

His mother's face clouded and he knew what was coming. The subject of Vaughn Knight always distressed her. Every time his name was brought up, she grew quiet. He suspected she'd postponed a promised visit to Hassie because, for whatever reason, she found it hard to talk about Vaughn. More than once he'd seen tears fill her eyes. His mother wasn't the only one; his father also tended to avoid conversations about Hassie's son. All Vaughn knew was that both his parents thought a great deal of the friend who'd lost his life in a rice paddy thirty-three years earlier. So much that it still caused them pain.

"I'm glad you're doing this," she said. "Over the years I've wanted to talk about Vaughn, but I get choked up whenever time I try."

She grabbed a bottle of hand lotion and occupied herself with that for a few moments, but Vaughn wasn't fooled. She didn't want him to see that her eyes were brimming with tears.

"Hassie will do a far better job of telling you about Vaughn than your father or I could."

Impulsively Vaughn hugged his mother, then joined his father, who was watching television in the living room.

On Sunday the drive into Buffalo Valley seemed to go faster than it had on Friday. He knew exactly where he needed to go, and the very landscape he'd found monotonous two days earlier now seemed familiar, even welcoming.

When he pulled into town, Buffalo Bob was spreading salt on the sidewalk in front of his own place and the businesses on either side. He waved, and Vaughn returned the gesture, then eased into a parking spot near the pharmacy. Once again he was struck by what an appealing town Buffalo Valley was. It felt as though he'd stepped back in time, to an era when family and a sense of community were priorities, when neighbor helped neighbor and people felt responsible for one another.

A sign on the door stated that the drugstore was open from noon until five on Sundays during December. When he walked inside, Vaughn found Hassie behind the counter. He automatically looked for Carrie and wasn't disappointed when he saw her over by the cash register, checking receipts. She paused in her task as soon as she saw him.

To his surprise, his mind had drifted toward her a number of times since Friday. He was attracted by her charm, which was real and uncontrived. She was genuine and warm, and he liked the pride in her eyes when she talked about her town.

She froze, as if she, too, had been thinking of him. That was a pleasant thought and one that sent a shiver of guilt through him. He was as good as engaged to Natalie, and the last thing he should be doing was flirting with another woman.

"Right on time," Hassie said, sounding much livelier this afternoon than she had two days earlier.

"I'm rarely tardy when I have a date with a beautiful woman," he teased, and watched both Hassie and Carrie smile. He generally didn't have much use for flattery, but occasionally it served a purpose. In this case, his rather silly statement had given everyone, including him, a moment of pleasure.

"You going to be all right here by yourself?" She turned to Carrie.

"Of course. You two go and visit, and don't you worry about a thing."

"I'll just get my coat," Hassie said, and disappeared to retrieve it. While she was gone, he had a few minutes with Carrie.

"I'm glad you're doing this for Hassie," she said. "It means so much to her to be sharing her son's life with you."

"I'm not doing it out of any sense of charity." Vaughn was truly interested in learning what he could about his namesake.

Hassie returned, wearing a long, dark coat, and they walked over to her house, which was one street off Main. Vaughn slowed his gait to match hers, tucking her arm in the crook of his elbow. Together they strolled leisurely down the newly shoveled sidewalk.

The house resembled something out of a 1950s movie. The furniture was large and bulky, covered in thick navy-blue fabric. Doilies decorated the back of the chair, and three were strategically placed across the back of the matching sofa. Even the television set was an old-fashioned floor model.

"It'll only take me a minute to make tea," Hassie announced heading toward the kitchen. He was given instructions to sit down and to look through the photo albums she'd already laid out.

Vaughn opened the biggest album. The first photograph he saw was a black-and-white version of a much younger Hassie standing with a baby cradled in her arms. A tall, handsome man stood awkwardly beside her, grinning self-consciously. His hand was on the shoulder of a little girl about four or five who stood in front of them, her dark brown hair in long braids.

Thereafter, photograph after photograph documented the life of Vaughn Knight. He was in Boy Scouts and active in his church. His school pictures showed increasing growth and maturity. When he reached high school, Vaughn had grown tall and athletic; a series of newspaper articles detailed his success on the basketball court and the football field. The year he was a senior, Buffalo Valley High School won the state football championship, with Vaughn Knight as the star quarterback. Another article named him Most Valuable Player.

His high-school graduation picture revealed the face of a young man eager to explore the world.

Hassie rejoined him, carrying a tray with a ceramic pot and two matching cups, as well as a plate of small cookies.

Vaughn stood and took the tray from her, placing it on the coffee table, and waited while she poured. He noticed that her hands were unsteady, but he didn't interrupt or try to assist her.

When she'd finished, she picked up a round, plain hatbox and removed the lid. "The top letter is the first one that mentions your mother."

Vaughn reached for the envelope.

September 30, 1966

Dear Mom and Dad,
I'm in love. Don't laugh when you read
this. Rick and I went to a hootenanny last
night and there was this terrific girl there.
Her name's Barbara Lowell, and guess
what? She's from Grand Forks. She's got
long blond hair and the most incredible
smile you've ever seen. After the
hootenanny we drank coffee and talked for
hours. I've never felt like this about any
other girl. She's smart and funny and so
beautiful I had a hard time not staring at
her. Even after I left her, I was so
wrapped up in meeting her I couldn't
sleep. First thing this morning, I called
her and we talked for two hours. Rick is
thoroughly disgusted with me and I don't
blame him, but I've never been in love before.

As soon as I can, I want to bring her
home for you to meet. You'll understand
why I feel the way I do once you see her
for yourselves.

Love,
Vaughn

"The Rick he's writing about is my dad?"
Vaughn asked.

Hassie nodded. "Here's another one you
might find interesting." She lifted a batch of

letters from the box. It was apparent from the way she sorted through the dates that she'd reread each letter countless times.

July 16, 1967

Dear Mom and Dad,
I've made my decision, but I have to tell you it was probably the most difficult I've ever had to make. I love Barb, and both of us want to get married right away. If I were thinking just of me, that's exactly what we'd do before I ship out. But I'm following your example, Dad. You and Mom waited until after the war to marry, and you came back safe and whole. I will, too.

Barb cried when I told her I felt it was best to delay the wedding until after my tour. Although you never advised me one way or the other, I had the feeling you thought it was better this way.

Vaughn stopped reading. "Did you want him to wait before marrying my mother?"

Hassie closed her eyes. "His father and I thought they were both too young. In the years that followed, I lived to regret that. Perhaps if Vaughn had married your mother, there might have been a grandchild. I realize that's terribly selfish, and I hope you'll forgive me."

"There's nothing to forgive."

"I always wondered if Jerry would've lived longer if we'd had grandchildren. Valerie was still in college at the time and wasn't married yet. A few years after that, she moved to Hawaii to take a job and met her husband there, but by then it was too late for Jerry."

"So your husband took the news of Vaughn's death very hard?"

"Once we received word about Vaughn, my husband was never the same. He was close to both children, but the shock of Vaughn's death somehow made him lose his emotional balance. Much as he loved Valerie and me, he couldn't get over the loss of his son. He went into a deep depression and started having heart problems. A year later, he died, too."

"Heart attack?"

"Technically, yes, but Vaughn's death is what really killed him, despite what that death certificate said. He simply gave up caring about anything. I wish . . ." Her voice trailed off.

"I'm sorry," Vaughn said, and meant it.

"Don't be." She patted his hand. "God knew better. Had your mother and my son married, you would never have been born."

It must have hit her hard that her son's fiancée and closest friend married each other within a year of his death. "Were you upset when my parents got married?" he asked.

"A little in the beginning, but then I realized that was exactly what Vaughn would have wanted. He did love her, and I know in my heart of hearts that she loved him, too."

"She did." Vaughn could say that without hesitation.

Hassie plucked a tissue from the nearby box and dabbed at her eyes. "I'd like you to have this." She reached for a second box and withdrew a heavy felt crest displaying the letters BVHS. It took Vaughn a moment to recognize that it was from a letterman's jacket.

"Vaughn was very proud of this. He earned it in wrestling. He was a natural at most sports. Basketball and football were barely a challenge, but that wasn't the case with wrestling. Many an afternoon he'd walk into the pharmacy and announce to his father and me that he was quitting. By dinnertime he'd change his mind and then he'd go back the next day." She paused, dabbing at her eyes again. "Our children were the very best of Jerry and me. Vaughn was a good son, and losing him changed all of us forever."

"I'd be honored to have this letter," Vaughn said.

"Thank you," Hassie whispered. She smiled faintly through her tears. "You must think me an old fool."

"No," he was quick to tell her. "I'm very glad you showed me all this." For the first time Vaughn Knight was more than a name, someone remembered who'd been lost in a war fought half a world away. He was alive in the words of his letters, in the photographs and in the heart of his mother.

"His letters from Vietnam are in this box," Hassie said. "They'll give you a feel for what it was like. If you're interested . . ."

Having served in the military, Vaughn was, of course, interested. He sat back and read the first letter. When he'd finally finished them all, it'd grown dark and Hassie was busy in the kitchen.

"What time is it?" he asked.

"It's after six."

"No." He found that hard to believe. "I had no idea I'd kept you this long. I apologize, Hassie. You should have stopped me."

She shook her head. "I couldn't. Your interest was a pleasure to me. Everything was fine with the store — Carrie's fully capable of handling anything that might come up. Besides, we're closed now."

"He could've been a writer, your son," Vaughn said, setting aside the last letter. For a few hours he'd been completely drawn into Vaughn Knight's descriptions of people and landscapes and events. Although the details were lightly sketched, a vivid picture of the young soldier's life had revealed itself through his words.

"I often thought that myself," Hassie agreed. After a brief silence she said, "I didn't want to interrupt you to ask about dinner. I hope it wasn't overly presumptuous to assume you'd join me."

"I'd like that very much."

Hassie nodded once, slowly, as if she considered his company of great worth.

While she put the finishing touches on the meal, Vaughn phoned his parents to tell them he'd be later than anticipated. "Be sure and give Hassie my love," his mother instructed. "Tell her your father and I plan to visit her soon."

"I will," he promised.

When he ended the phone conversation, he found Hassie setting the table. He insisted on taking over, eager to contribute something to their dinner. His admiration and love for the older woman had grown this afternoon in ways he hadn't thought possible on such short acquaintance. She'd opened his eyes to a couple of important things. First and foremost, he'd learned about the man he'd been named after and discovered he had quite a lot to live up to. Second, he'd come to see his parents in a new light. He understood how their fallen friend had shaped their lives and their marriage. It was no wonder they didn't often speak of Vaughn Knight. The years might have dulled the pain, but the sense of loss was as strong in them as it was in Hassie.

They chatted over dinner, and his mood

lightened. Hassie was wise and considerate; she seemed to understand how serious his thoughts had become.

"The community is lighting the Christmas tree this evening," she said casually as Vaughn carried their dishes to the sink.

"Are you going?" he asked.

"I wouldn't miss it for the world," Hassie informed him. "The Christmas tree is set up beside the War Memorial. Nearly everyone in town will be there —" she paused and looked at him "— including Carrie."

"Are you playing matchmaker with me, Hassie Knight?" he asked. He had a feeling she didn't miss much — and that she'd seen the way his gaze had been drawn to Carrie when he'd entered the pharmacy.

Hassie chuckled. "She's smitten, you know."

Smitten. What a wonderful old-fashioned word, Vaughn mused. It would take a better man than him not to feel flattered.

"You could do worse."

"And how do you know I don't already have a girlfriend waiting for me in Seattle?" he asked, and wondered what Hassie would think of Natalie. For some reason he had the impression she wouldn't think much of her sharp-edged sophistication. It'd taken him a while to see past Natalie's polished exterior; once he had, he'd realized she was just like everyone else, trying to be noticed and to make a name for herself.

"You don't," Hassie returned confidently.

He was about to tell her about Natalie, when Hassie said, "Come with me. Come and watch the community tree being lit. There's no better way to learn about Buffalo Valley."

Vaughn's purpose, other than meeting Hassie, was to do exactly that. Still, seeing Carrie again appealed to him, too — more than it should.

"That's just what I need to put me in the Christmas spirit," Vaughn said. "I'd consider it an honor to accompany you."

"Wonderful." Hassie clasped her hands together as though to keep herself from clapping with delight. "I can't tell you how happy this makes me."

He helped her on with her coat, then grabbed his own. Taking her arm again, Vaughn guided her out the door and down the front steps. By the time they rounded the corner to Main Street and the City Park, the town was coming to life. There were groups of people converging on the park and cars stopping here and there. The air was filled with festivity — carols played over a loudspeaker, kids shrieking excitedly, shouts of welcome . . . and laughter everywhere. Vaughn could practically *feel* the happiness all around him.

"This is about as close as it gets to a traffic jam in Buffalo Valley," Hassie told him.

As soon as they appeared, it seemed everyone in town called a greeting to Hassie.
Vaughn had never seen anything to compare
with the reverence and love people obviously
felt for her.

"You've been holding out on me, Hassie
Knight," an older man teased as he approached. "I didn't realize I had competi-
tion."

"Cut it out, Joshua McKenna." Hassie
grinned. "Meet Vaughn Kyle."

"Mighty pleased to meet you." The man
thrust out his hand for Vaughn to shake.

"Nearly everyone in a fifty-mile radius is
coming," Joshua said, glancing around him.
More and more cars arrived, and the park
was actually getting crowded.

"I don't see Calla. She's not going to make
it home this year?"

"And miss spoiling her baby brother?"
Joshua returned. "You're joking, right?"

Hassie laughed delightedly. "I should have
known better."

"Jeb, Maddy and the kids are already
here."

The names flew over Vaughn's head, but it
was apparent that Hassie loved each family.

"Maddy owns the grocery," Joshua explained as they strolled across the street and
entered the park. "She's married to my son.
Best thing that ever happened to him."

"Oh, yes — I saw the grocery," Vaughn

said. "Maddy. I remember. The fantastic reindeer."

Joshua grinned widely. "Yup, that's our Maddy. Loves any excuse to decorate — and does a great job."

"They have two of the most precious children you'll ever want to see," Hassie added, "with another on the way."

"The first pregnancy and this latest one were real surprises."

"I'll bet Jeb's developed a liking for blizzards," Hassie murmured, and the two older folks burst into laughter.

"You'd have to know the history of that family to understand what's so amusing," Carrie said, joining them.

"Hello again," Vaughn murmured.

"Hi."

Vaughn had trouble looking away.

"How about you and Carrie getting me some hot chocolate?" the older woman asked.

"Bring some for me, too, while you're at it," Joshua said.

"I think we just got our marching orders," Carrie told him, her eyes smiling. "Is that okay?"

"I don't mind if you don't," Vaughn replied.

The cold had brought color to her cheeks, and her long blond hair straggled out from under her wool hat. "It's fine with me. Buffalo Bob and Merrily are serving cocoa and cookies over there," she said a little breath-lessly.

"I'll be right back," Vaughn said over his shoulder as he followed Carrie.

"Don't rush," Hassie called after him . . . and then he thought he saw her wink at him.

Chapter 3

The Christmas lights strung around the outside of the old house welcomed Vaughn back to his parents' home. His mother had been born and raised in Grand Forks, but his grandparents had moved to Arizona when he was six. Vaughn had no recollection of visiting the Dakotas, although he was certain they had. His memories centered on the Denver area and his father's family. Not until Rick was accepted for early retirement did they decide to return to the home that had been in the Lowell family for more than a hundred years.

The television blared from the living room as Vaughn let himself into the house, entering through the door off the kitchen after stomping the snow from his shoes on the back porch. He unzipped his jacket and hung it on a peg, along with his muffler.

"Is that you, Vaughn?" his mother called.

"No, it's Santa," he joked.

He watched as his mother, still holding her needlepoint, hurried into the kitchen. "You're not hungry, are you?"

"I filled up on cookies and hot chocolate."

His mother studied him as if to gauge how the meeting with Hassie had gone — the *real* question she wanted to ask, he suspected. "Did you have a . . . good visit?"

"Yes." He nodded reassuringly. "We talked before dinner, but afterward there was a tree-lighting ceremony in the park."

"You attended that?" His mother sounded pleased.

"Sure, why not?" His response was flippant, as though this was the very thing he'd normally do. In truth, though, Vaughn couldn't recall attending anything like it since he was in grade school. The evening had been quite an experience. The whole town had come alive with music and laughter and people enjoying one another's company. Christmas had never been a big deal to Vaughn — but he'd never seen an entire community join together like this, either. He knew it had made a lasting impression on him, that it left him longing for the same kind of warmth. For a true spirit of celebration, far removed from sophisticated parties and decorator-trimmed trees.

"How is Hassie?" his mother asked.

Vaughn wasn't sure what to say. Hassie was without a doubt one of the most dynamic women he'd ever met. She possessed character and depth and a heart that poured out love for her family and her community. He'd immediately seen how deeply she was loved and respected. After these hours in her company, Vaughn had understood why. "She's an extraordinary woman."

"I know." His mother's voice was soft, a little tentative. Before Vaughn could say more, she'd retreated into the living room.

Vaughn followed and his father muted the television, obviously waiting for him to enlighten them about his visit.

"Hassie let me read the letters her son wrote from Vietnam."

His mother resumed her needlepoint and lowered her head, as though the stitches demanded her full attention.

"They were riveting. I learned about the war itself, things I could never have learned from a book, and about the man who wrote them." At the time, Hassie's son had been younger than Vaughn was now. In his letters, Vaughn had recognized the other man's sense of humanity, his hatred of war and his desire to make a difference, to share in a struggle for freedom.

"We met at the University of Michigan during our freshman year of college," his father said, and his eyes went blank. He seemed to be back in a different place, a different time. Vaughn knew he hadn't been accepted into the service himself because of poor eyesight. "He was my roommate. Both of us were away from home for the first time and in an environment completely foreign and unfamiliar. I suppose it's only natural that we became close."

His mother added in a low voice, "He was the most generous person I've ever known."

"He got a part-time job tutoring a youngster who had leukemia," his father continued, his gaze focused on the television screen. "He was hired for three hours a week, but Vaughn spent much more time with him than that. He played games with Joey, talked to him, cheered him up, and when Joey died at thirteen, the boy's mother said Vaughn had been his best friend."

"That's the kind of person he was," his mother said.

"Hassie gave me the school letter he earned in wrestling. And then, after I walked her back home, she said there was something else she wanted me to have." His parents looked up when he paused. Even now, Vaughn could hardly believe Hassie would give him such a gift.

"What, son?"

"Her husband's gold pocket watch. It would've been Vaughn's had he lived." Hassie had placed it in his hands with tears filming her eyes, then closed his fingers around it.

"Treasure it, Vaughn," his mother whispered.

"I do." Vaughn's first reaction had been to refuse something that was clearly a valuable family heirloom, something that meant a great deal to the old woman. He'd felt the significance of her gift and was moved by the solemnity of her words and gestures when she'd presented it to him.

He would always keep it safe. And he would pass it down to his oldest son or daughter.

"What else did Hassie tell you?" his father asked.

"She . . . said how much Vaughn had loved Mom."

"He did."

Vaughn studied his father, looking for any sign of jealousy. If he'd been in his father's shoes — well, he wasn't entirely sure *how* he'd feel.

"We planned to marry," his mother said, "but Hassie probably told you that."

He nodded. "She showed me the letter in which Vaughn explains why it would be best to wait until he returned from Vietnam."

"Only, he didn't return. And everything worked out in a completely different way." His mother took his father's hand and held it and they gazed at each other for a moment. "But a good way," she said quietly.

"I often wondered what Hassie really thought about the two of us getting married," his father said. He stared at Vaughn as if, after meeting Hassie, he could supply the answer.

Indeed, Vaughn had seen the look that

came over her face when she mentioned his parents' marriage. "At first I think she took it hard." This didn't appear to surprise either of his parents.

"Our marriage was a reminder that Vaughn was never coming home," his mother said, "and that no matter how much pain the world brings us, life continues."

"She said as much herself."

"I think . . . she was disappointed in us both."

"Perhaps in the beginning," Vaughn agreed, "but she changed her mind later. She told me she felt that her son approved."

"I'm sure he did," his mother whispered.

His father reached abruptly for the remote, indicating that the conversation was over. Sound flared back, and Vaughn got up and went to the kitchen to pour himself a cup of coffee before rejoining his parents.

"Oh, dear, I almost forgot to tell you," his mother said. "Natalie phoned."

Vaughn's first reaction was that he didn't want to talk to her. Not tonight. Not after such an emotionally overwhelming day. Knowing Natalie, she'd want to discuss business, and that was the last thing on his mind. He needed to think before he returned the call, needed to absorb what he'd learned first — about the town, about Hassie . . . about himself.

"It isn't too late to call her back," his

mother said. "With the time difference, it's barely eight on the West Coast."

"I know," he said absently, his thoughts now on Carrie Hendrickson. Much of the evening had been spent with her. After they'd brought hot chocolate to Hassie and Joshua McKenna, she'd introduced him to her family.

Vaughn had seen the wary look in her brothers' eyes and realized how protective they were of her. He wished he'd had more of a chance to talk to Carrie, but they were constantly interrupted. She was a favorite with her nieces and nephews, who were forever running up to her, involving her in their games and their squabbles. She was a natural peacemaker, he observed, one of those people whose very presence brought out the best impulses in others. Like Hassie. And the people in town valued Carrie in much the same way; that was easy to tell. They came to her for advice and comfort. They were drawn to her just as he was.

"Your father and I are looking forward to meeting Natalie," his mother said, breaking into his musings.

Vaughn started guiltily. He was as good as engaged — although, he supposed, all they'd really done was discuss the possibility of marriage. He hadn't divulged his plans to either of his parents. At Natalie's request, he hadn't even told them about his job. "She's

70

anxious to meet you, too," he said, but without a lot of enthusiasm. The contrast between Natalie and Carrie flashed like a neon sign in his brain. One was warm and personable and focused on the needs of her community, the other sharp, savvy and ambitious. When he'd arrived in North Dakota, he thought he knew what he wanted; all at once, he wasn't sure.

"You've been seeing her for two years now," his mother went on, watching him.

"Barbara, the boy doesn't need you to tell him that."

Vaughn sipped his coffee. This was one conversation he had no wish to continue. "Carrie and I are going Christmas shopping tomorrow," he said, instead.

His mother lowered the needlepoint to her lap and stared at him. "Carrie? Who's Carrie?"

Vaughn didn't realize his mistake until it was too late. "A friend."

His mother raised her eyebrows as if his answer didn't please her. "When did you have time to make friends?"

"She works with Hassie at the pharmacy."

"I see." It appeared his mother did see, because she said nothing more.

Vaughn wished he understood his own feelings. A week ago he would have rushed to return Natalie's call. He wasn't avoiding *her,* he decided, but the subject of Value-X and

71

Buffalo Valley. In a matter of days — one day, really — he'd become oddly protective of the town . . . and its people. Hassie, of course, but Carrie, too. Natalie was bound to ask him questions he no longer wanted to answer.

One thing was clear; he needed to think the situation through very carefully.

Craving solitude, Vaughn swallowed the last of his coffee, then announced he was heading for bed.

His mother glanced up at the wall clock. "Aren't you calling Natalie?"

He frowned. "Later. Don't worry about it, Mom."

"Vaughn has to rest up for shopping," his father teased.

"Ah yes, the great shopping expedition. Where will it be, by the way?"

"The mall here in town."

"You're actually going to a mall at this time of year?" His father looked at him as though he'd lost his sanity.

Vaughn gave a nonchalant shrug. He didn't know what had possessed him to suggest he and Carrie meet at Columbia Mall. His excuse had been that Carrie was a wonderful source of information about the town. He'd never had the opportunity to bring up the subject of Value-X, and wanted to get her reactions to it. Or so he told himself.

The truth was, he wanted to know her better.

Hassie sat up in bed, her eyes on the photograph of her son on the bedroom wall. She looked at Jerry's picture next and Valerie's, then turned back to Vaughn's. It was only natural that she'd be thinking about her son tonight.

Time passed with such inexorable swiftness, she reflected. She had startlingly clear memories of Vaughn as a toddler, stumbling toward her, arms outstretched. If she closed her eyes, she could almost hear his laughter. She'd loved to scoop him into her arms and hug him close until he squirmed, wanting to run and play with his older sister. As they grew older, Valerie had listened to his confidences and offered a big sister's sage advice.

How carefree life had been for her and Jerry in the early 1950s. Simple pleasures had meant a great deal back then. She could think of no greater comfort than sitting with her husband after a day at the pharmacy, a day they'd spent working together. Jerry would slip his arm around her shoulder and she'd press her head against his. He loved to whisper the sweetest words in her ear, and oh, she'd enjoyed being in his arms. In those days, it seemed the sun would never stop shining and the world would always be filled with happiness.

Turning out the light, Hassie nestled under the covers and let her memories take her back. Valerie and Vaughn used to come to the pharmacy every afternoon after school. To this day she could still picture the two of them sitting at the soda fountain, waiting to be served an after-school snack. They were a normal sister and brother, constantly bickering. Valerie always teased Vaughn, and when she did, he'd tug her pigtails hard enough to bring tears to her eyes. Then it would be up to Hassie to chastise them both. Softhearted Jerry had left the discipline to her. Hassie hated it, but knew her children needed to understand that their actions had consequences.

The years flew by so fast! Looking back, Hassie wished she'd appreciated each day a little more, treasured each moment with her children while they were young. Before she could account for all the years that had passed, it was 1960, and Vaughn was in high school.

Jerry was especially proud of Vaughn's athletic talent. He, too, had been a sports star in his youth. Vaughn had played team sports throughout his four years in high school, and they'd never missed a game. One or the other, and often both of them, were at his games, even if it meant closing the pharmacy, although they didn't do that often. They always sat in the same section of the stands so

Vaughn would know where to find them. When his team came onto the field, it wasn't unusual for him to turn toward the bleachers and survey the crowd until he located his parents. Then he'd smile and briefly raise one hand.

Without even trying, Hassie could hear the crowds and recall the cheerleaders' triumphant leaps, while the school band played in the background.

Watching Vaughn play ball had been hard on Hassie's nerves. Twice that she could remember, her son had been injured. Both times Jerry had to stop her from running onto the field. She stood with the other concerned parents, her hands over her mouth, as the coaches assessed his injuries. On both occasions Vaughn had walked off the playing field unaided, but it'd been pride that had carried him. The first time his arm had been broken, and the second, his nose.

His high-school years had been wonderful. The girls always had eyes for Vaughn. Not only was he a star athlete and academically accomplished, he was tall and good-looking. The phone nearly rang off the hook during his junior and senior years. There'd never been anyone special, though, until he met Barbara Lowell in college. She'd been his first love and his last.

Hassie recalled how handsome he'd looked in his brand-new suit for the junior-senior

75

prom, although he'd been uncomfortable in the starched white dress shirt. The photo from the dance revealed how ill at ease he'd been. His expression, Jerry had said, was that of someone who expected to be hit by a water balloon.

Hassie had suggested he ask Theresa Burkhart to the biggest dance of the year. He'd done so, but he'd never asked her out for a second date. When Hassie asked him why, Vaughn shrugged and had nothing more to say. Every afternoon for a week after the prom, Theresa had stopped at the soda fountain, obviously hoping to run into Vaughn. Each afternoon she left, looking disappointed.

Packing Vaughn's suitcase the day before he went off to the University of Michigan was another fond memory. She'd lovingly placed his new clothes in the suitcase that would accompany him on this first trip away from home. Although saddened by his departure, she took comfort in knowing he'd only be gone for a few years. This wasn't a new experience, since Valerie had left four years earlier and was attending Oregon State. She was working part-time and seemed in no particular hurry to finish her education. Jerry and Hassie had been reassured by Vaughn's promise to return as a pharmacist himself. He shared their commitment to community and their belief in tradition.

Soon the kitchen table was littered with his

letters home. The letter in which he first mentioned meeting Barbara had brought back memories of Hassie's own — like meeting Jerry at college just before the war. The day that letter arrived, she'd sat at the kitchen table with her husband and they'd held hands and reminisced about the early days of their own romance.

Then the unthinkable happened. News of a war in a country she'd barely heard of escalated daily. The papers, television and radio were filled with reports, despite President Johnson's promises to limit the United States' involvement. Then the day came when Vaughn phoned home and announced, like so many young men his age, that he'd been drafted. A numbness had spread from Hassie's hand and traveled up her arm. It didn't stop until it had reached her heart. Vaughn was going to war. Like his father before him, he would carry a rifle and see death.

This wasn't supposed to happen. For a while, men in college were exempt, but with the war's escalation, they were now included. Vaughn took the news well, but not Hassie. He had to do his part, he told her. It was too easy to pass the burden onto someone else. Citizenship came with a price tag.

Suddenly bombs were exploding all around her. Terrified, Hassie hid her head in her hands, certain she was about to die. Bullets whizzed past her and she gasped, her heart cramping with a terrible fear. All at once she was cold, colder than she could ever remember being, and then she was flat on her back with the sure knowledge that she'd been hit. The sky was an intense shade of blue, and she was simultaneously lying there and hovering far above. But when she looked down, it wasn't her face she saw. It was the face of her dying son. His blood drained out of him with unstoppable speed as the frantic medic worked over him.

Her son, the child of her heart, was dying. He saw her and tried to smile, to tell her it was all right, but his eyes closed and he was gone. Her baby was forever gone.

A crushing load of grief weighed on Hassie's heart. She cried out and, groaning, sat upright.

It was then she realized she'd fallen asleep. This had all been a dream. Awash with memories, she'd drifted into a dream so real she could hear the fading echoes of exploding ammunition as she dragged herself out of a past world and back to reality.

As her eyes adjusted to the dark, her gaze darted from one familiar object to another. From the bedroom door where her housecoat hung on a hook to the dresser top with the silver mirror and brush set Jerry had given her on their tenth anniversary.

"Vaughn." His name was a broken whisper,

and she realized that she couldn't remember what he looked like. His face, so well loved, refused to come. Strain as she might, she couldn't see him. Panic descended, and she tossed aside the blankets and slid out of bed. It wasn't her son's image that filled her mind, but the face of another young man. Another Vaughn.

Vaughn Kyle.

"Of course," she whispered, clutching the bedpost. Leaning against it, she heaved a deep, quivering sigh and climbed back into bed.

Wrapping the quilt around her, she tucked her arm beneath her pillow and closed her eyes. Yes, it made sense that she'd dream of Vaughn that night. Her Vaughn. It also made sense that it was Vaughn Kyle's face she now saw. After all, she'd spent much of the day with him.

Barbara and Rick had done a good job raising him. Vaughn was a fine man, honest and genuine, sensitive yet forthright. She was grateful she'd had the opportunity to meet him before she died.

Giving him the gold watch had been a spur-of-the-moment decision. It was the one possession of Jerry's she'd held back from Valerie and her two granddaughters. Valerie lived in Hawaii and although they were close, they rarely visited each other. Hassie had flown to the island once, but all those tourists and hordes of people had made her nervous. Not only that, she wasn't comfortable in planes, and the long flight made her nervous. A few years back, after a scare with Hassie's heart, Valerie had flown out to spend time with her, but had soon grown bored and restless.

Hassie didn't think Val's daughters, Alison and Charlotte, would have much interest in their grandfather's watch. But it was precious to her, so she'd kept it.

She knew when she pressed the watch into Vaughn's palm that this was the right thing to do. He looked as if he was about to argue with her, but he didn't and she was glad. Still, his hesitation told her more clearly than any words that he understood the significance of her gift.

Warm once more, Hassie stretched out her legs, enjoying the feel of the sheets against her bare skin. She smiled, remembering the exchange she'd witnessed between Carrie and Vaughn Kyle last night. She hoped something came of it. After her divorce Carrie was understandably wary about relationships, but Hassie felt confident that Vaughn would never intentionally do anything to hurt her.

"Can't something be done?" Carrie asked, pacing in front of Heath Quantrill's polished wood desk. As the president of Buffalo Valley Bank, he just might know of some way to stop Value-X from moving into town. In the past day or so, news of the retailer's plans had spread through town faster than an August brushfire. Carrie had first heard of it that morning. She suspected Hassie knew and had been protecting her; she also suspected there'd been rumors last night, but she'd been too involved with Vaughn to notice.

Heath's frown darkened. It went without saying that he wasn't any happier about this than she was. "I'm sorry, Carrie, but Ambrose Kohn is a difficult man to deal with. The town council has spoken to him several times. Hassie tried and I did, too, but he isn't willing to listen."

"You knew before this morning?" she fired back. "Hassie, too?" That was what she thought — and it explained a great deal. Hassie just hadn't been herself lately, but every inquiry was met with denial.

Heath nodded.

"Doesn't Mr. Kohn realize what he's doing?" Carrie found it hard to believe he could be so callous toward the town.

"He knows all too well."

"People have a right to know that the entire future of our town is at risk." She could only imagine what would happen to her father's store if Value-X set up shop.

Heath obviously agreed with her. "Hassie suggested we keep this under wraps until after Christmas, and the rest of the council decided to go along with her. I don't know how the news leaked." He scowled and rolled his gold pen between flat palms.

Delaying the bad news changed nothing. This morning at breakfast her father had announced what he'd learned. He was already alternating between depression and panic. He'd heard it from Joanie Wyatt at the tree-lighting ceremony. The Wyatts had sent away for stock information, and Joanie had read over a prospectus; she'd immediately seen that Buffalo Valley was listed as a possible expansion site. She'd immediately phoned Buffalo Bob, who'd reluctantly confirmed it.

"Nothing's been signed yet," Heath said, as though that should make her feel better. It didn't.

She glanced at her watch, wishing she had more time to get all this straight in her mind. Although she was eager to meet Vaughn at the Columbia Mall as promised, she wasn't in the mood for Christmas activities. Not with this Value-X problem hanging over all their heads.

"Have you talked to anyone at the corporate office?" she asked.

Heath nodded.

"They weren't interested in listening, were they?" Heath's disheartened look was answer enough. "It's *progress*, right?"

"Right," Heath muttered. "Listen, I've got

a meeting in ten minutes. I'm sorry, Carrie. I know what this will mean for your father's business and Knight's Pharmacy, too. I'm doing the best I can."

"Can't you buy the property yourself?"

"I approached Kohn about that, but . . ."

"He won't sell it to you?" Carrie asked in an outraged voice.

"Let's say he'd love a bidding war — one I'd be sure to lose." Heath stood and retrieved his overcoat from a closet.

Her gaze pleaded with his. "You've *got* to find a way to keep Value-X out of Buffalo Valley."

"Kohn hasn't heard the last of this," Heath promised as he escorted her out of the bank.

Carrie accompanied him to his four-wheel-drive vehicle.

"Is there anything *I* can do?" she asked, feeling the need to act.

Heath shook his head as he opened his car door. "Don't worry, Carrie, this isn't over yet. Not by a long shot."

All Carrie could do was trust that, somehow or other, he'd convince Ambrose Kohn to be reasonable.

The drive into Grand Forks passed in a fog. Burdened by the news, Carrie was surprised when the two lanes widened to four as she reached the outskirts of the big city.

Vaughn was waiting for her inside the mall at a coffee shop they'd designated as their meeting place. He stood as she approached. She was struck again by what an attractive man he was. Her ex-husband had been attractive, too, but Alec's good looks had belied his selfish, arrogant nature. She'd learned, the hard way, that a handsome face proved nothing about the inner man. No, handsome is as handsome does, her grandma always said. Which made Vaughn Kyle very handsome, indeed.

He'd been so gentle and caring with Hassie. He'd spent time with her, listened to her talk about her son. Carrie marveled at his patience and his good humor and the respect he seemed to genuinely feel for Hassie and for the town. When he'd asked her to meet him in Grand Forks to help him finish his shopping, she'd agreed. It'd been a long, long time since a man had impressed her as much as Vaughn Kyle.

"Thanks for coming," he said now.

Although it was relatively early, the mall was already frantic. With exactly a week left before Christmas, the entire population of Grand Forks had apparently decided to cram itself inside.

"The only person I still need to buy for is my mother," he told her, looking around as though he already regretted this.

"What about perfume?" Carrie wasn't feeling too inspired, either.

"She's allergic to a lot of those scents."

"Okay, how about . . ." Carrie proceeded to rattle off several other suggestions, all of which he categorically dismissed for one reason or another.

"Do you have any more ideas?" he asked, looking desperate.

"Not yet, but we might stumble across something while we're here."

Vaughn sighed. "That doesn't sound promising." He glanced around. "How about if we find a quiet restaurant and discuss it over lunch?"

He didn't need to ask twice. She was as anxious to get away from the crowds as he was. They found an Italian place Joanie and Brandon Wyatt had once recommended and were seated almost immediately. Sitting at their table with its red-and-white-checkered tablecloth, Carrie could see why her friends liked it here. The casual atmosphere was perfect. If the food was half as good as the smells wafting from the kitchen, she was in for a treat.

Carrie quickly made her decision and closed the menu. Lowering her gaze, she pushed thoughts of Value-X from her mind for the umpteenth time. Her worries kept intruding on the pleasant day she was hoping to have.

"You'd better tell me," Vaughn said. His hand reached for hers and he gently squeezed it. "Something's wrong."

Apparently she hadn't done a very good job of hiding her concerns. Rather than blurt everything out, she stared down at the table-cloth for a long moment.

"We learned this morning that Value-X is considering Buffalo Valley as a possible site," she finally said. "Apparently they've already negotiated for a piece of land. I don't need to tell you what that'll do to our community."

"It might be a good thing," he said slowly. "Try to think positive."

"If this is progress, we don't want anything to do with it," she muttered. Vaughn couldn't *possibly* understand. She was sorry she'd brought up the subject. "We happen to like our town just the way it is."

"It isn't that —"

"We're going to fight it," she said confidently.

"How?" Vaughn asked. "Isn't that a little like David fighting Goliath?"

"Perhaps, but like David, you can bet we aren't going to idly sit by and do nothing." Already plans had started to form in her mind. "Other communities have succeeded. We can, too."

"You're serious about this?"

"Damn straight I am."

"Don't you think you're overlooking the positive aspects of a company like Value-X opening a store in Buffalo Valley? They have a lot to offer."

Carrie glared at him. "You don't get it, do you?"

"I guess not. Help me understand." Vaughn leaned back in his chair, his expression serious.

"Value-X will ruin *everything*. We don't want it, we don't need it." Carrie struggled to keep her voice even.

Vaughn studied her. "I imagine you're a formidable opponent when you put your mind to something."

"It isn't only me," she told him. "The entire town is up in arms. We haven't come this far to let some heartless enterprise wipe out all our efforts."

Vaughn frowned. "Value-X will mean the end of Knight's Pharmacy, won't it?"

That was only the beginning as far as Carrie could tell. "And AceMan Hardware." She ran one finger across the tines of the fork. "The only business I can't see it affecting is the Buffalo Valley Quilting Company." Carrie shot him a look and wondered why she hadn't thought of this earlier. "That's it!"

"What is?"

"A quilt. It's the perfect Christmas gift for your mother."

Vaughn didn't appear convinced. "A quilt?"

"They're special. Hand-sewn, and you could go traditional or innovative."

"How much are they?"

"I don't know the full range of prices," she said, "but if the quilt is more than you want to spend, there're table runners and place mats and lap robes."

"Hmm." The idea seemed to take hold. "That does sound like a gift she'd enjoy."

"I'm sure she would," Carrie said. "I can't believe I didn't think of it earlier."

"So how do I go about this?"

"If you don't want to drive back to Buffalo Valley so soon, I could choose one for you," she offered.

"Perhaps Mom should pick it out herself."

"Great idea — and I know Hassie would love to see her."

"I think it would do my mother a world of good to renew her friendship with Hassie."

The waitress arrived and took their orders. Seafood linguine for her, lasagna for him. And a glass of red wine for each. "Hey, it's Christmas," Vaughn said with a grin.

He took his cell phone from his jacket and flipped it open. Within seconds, he had his mother on the line.

"What about tomorrow?" he asked, looking at Carrie.

"I'm sure that'll be fine."

"Hassie will be there, won't she?"

Carrie nodded. "She's scheduled to work in the morning, but she has the afternoon free. I'll cover for her, if need be."

He relayed the information to his mother,

then ended the conversation and slid the phone back inside his jacket. Smiling at her, he said, "Thanks, Carrie."

A warm feeling came over her, and once again she lowered her gaze. Vaughn Kyle — kind to old women and a thoughtful son. He was exciting and he was interesting and he made her heart beat furiously. She could only regret that he was heading back to Seattle so soon after Christmas.

Chapter 4

"I suppose you heard," Hassie said when Leta Betts came bustling into the pharmacy late in the afternoon. The word about Value-X had filtered through Buffalo Valley, and the town was rife with speculation. Nearly everyone she knew had stopped by to talk it over with her, as though she had a solution to this perplexing problem.

"I don't like it," Leta muttered, walking behind the counter of the soda fountain and pulling out a well-used teapot. "Want me to make you a cup?"

"Please." Hassie had filled prescriptions all afternoon, between interruptions, and she was ready for a break. She'd known that Leta would come by at some point; fortunately, there was a lull just now, which made it a good time to talk to her dearest friend.

"Where's Carrie?" Leta found two mugs and set them on the counter.

"It's her day off."

"I heard she went to see Heath."

Hassie had heard about that, as well. Carrie had a good heart and cared about this community with the same intensity as Hassie did. Once Carrie received her Pharm.D., Hassie had planned to turn the business over to her. That was before the threat of Value-X, however. If that threat became a reality, Hassie couldn't sell the pharmacy, not in good conscience. In all likelihood the place would be out of business within a year after the big retailer moved in.

"It's a shame, you know," Leta murmured. She dragged a chair closer to the counter and perched on the seat. Leaning forward, she braced her elbows on the edge, sighing deeply. "Who'd have thought something like this would ever happen?"

Hassie shook her head helplessly. She'd worked so hard to save this town. And now, even if oblivion wasn't to be its fate, a corporation like Value-X could make Buffalo Valley unrecognizable, could turn it into something that bore no resemblance to the place it had been. The place it *should* be.

"What are we going to do?" Leta asked.

Hassie sat next to her and assumed the same slouched pose. Leta was her friend and employee, and there wasn't anything Hassie couldn't tell her. But this situation with the conglomerate had her poleaxed. She was at her wit's end. "I don't know," she admitted.

"We'll think of something," Leta insisted, and poured tea into the mugs. She set one in front of Hassie and then added a teaspoon of sugar to her own.

"Not this time," Hassie said as she reached for the mug, letting it warm her hands. She was too old and too tired. A few years back she'd fought for her town with determination and ingenuity, but this new war would have to be waged by someone else. She'd done her part.

"This was how we both felt when we learned Lindsay had decided to return to Atlanta, remember?" Leta prodded.

As though Hassie would ever forget. At the last minute Leta's son, Gage, had realized he'd be making the worst mistake of his life if he let Lindsay leave without telling her how much he loved her. As a result, Lindsay had not only stayed on as a high-school teacher, she'd married Gage. Leta was a grandmother twice over, thanks to the young couple.

"Value-X is too powerful for me." A bit of research had revealed that the retailer was accustomed to exactly this kind of local resistance. They had their battle plans worked out to the smallest detail. Hassie remembered from the television exposé that the company had a legal team, as well as public-relations people, all of them experts at squelching opposition. Hassie knew the town council couldn't afford any high-priced attorneys to plead their case. Even if they banded together, they were no match for the company's corporate attorneys. They were cut-throat, they'd seen it all, done it all. According to the documentary, they'd won in the majority of their cases. Like it or not, Value-X simply overran a community.

"We can't give up," Leta insisted. She glared at Hassie, as though waiting for some of the old fight to surface.

It wouldn't, though. Not anymore. Slowly Hassie lowered her gaze, refusing to meet her friend's eyes. "It's a lost cause," she murmured.

"This doesn't sound like you, Hassie."

"No," she agreed, glancing at her tired reflection in the mirror above the soda fountain, "but it won't matter that much if I lose the pharmacy."

Leta's jaw sagged open. "Wh-what —"

"I should've retired years ago. The only reason I held on as long as I did is the community needs a pharmacy and —"

"What about Carrie?"

Hassie had been so pleased and grateful when Carrie had come to work as an intern. This was what she'd always wanted for the pharmacy. Years ago she'd expected her son to take over, but Vietnam had robbed her of that dream. The hopelessness of the situation settled squarely over her heart.

"I'm sure Value-X will require a pharmacist. Carrie can apply there."

Silent, Leta stared into the distance.

"I'm tired," Hassie said. "Valerie's been after

93

me to retire, move to Hawaii. . . .   Maybe I should."

"You in Hawaii? Never!" Leta shook her head fiercely. "I've always followed your lead — we all have. I don't know what would've become of us if not for you."

"Fiddlesticks." Hassie forced a laugh. "Value-X is coming to town, and that's all there is to it. We might as well accept the inevitable. Not long from now, both of us will be shopping there and wondering how we ever lived without such a store in town."

"You're probably right," Leta returned, but her words rang false.

"Let's just enjoy Christmas," Hassie suggested, gesturing at the garlands strung from the old-fashioned ceiling lights. "What are your plans?"

"Kevin won't be home, but he'll call from Paris on Christmas Eve. Gage and Lindsay invited me to spend Christmas Day with them." Hassie knew that Leta would take delight in spoiling four-year-old Joy and two-year-old Madeline.

"Bob and Merrily invited me over in the morning to open gifts with them and Bobby," Hassie told her friend. They thought of her as Bobby's unofficial grandmother. Early in their marriage, Bob and Merrily had lost a son — although not to death. They'd fostered a child from an abusive environment and had wanted to adopt him, but in the end, the

California authorities had seen fit to place the boy with another family. It'd been a difficult time for the couple. Having lost a son herself, Hassie had understood their grief as only someone who'd walked that path could understand it. She'd tried to bring them comfort and the example of her endurance. Bob and Merrily never forgot her kindness, little as it was. Over the past few years, they'd become as close to her as family.

"You finally met Vaughn Kyle," Leta said. "That's definitely a highlight of this Christmas season."

"Yes," Hassie agreed, somewhat cheered. It'd been an unanticipated pleasure, one she'd always remember. In the hours they'd spent with each other, she'd forged a bond with the young man. Meeting Vaughn had left Hassie feeling closer to her own son, although he'd been dead for thirty-three years. Hard to believe so much time had passed since his death. . . .

"That was him with Carrie at the tree-lighting ceremony, wasn't it?"

Hassie felt a small, sudden joy, sending a ray of light into the gloom she'd experienced earlier. "She's spending the afternoon with him in Grand Forks."

"It's time she put the divorce behind her."

Hassie felt the same way but didn't comment.

"Do you think something might come of

95

it?" Leta asked, her voice slightly raised.

Hassie couldn't answer. Her hours with Vaughn had been taken up with the past, and she hadn't discovered much at all about his future plans. She knew he'd been honorably discharged from the military and had accepted a position with a Seattle-based company, although he'd never said which one. Probably a big software firm, she decided. From what she understood, he'd be starting work after the first of the year. She felt it was a good sign that he'd come to spend two weeks with his parents.

"He's been to town twice already," Leta offered. "That's encouraging, don't you think?"

"I suppose."

A small smile quivered at the edges of Leta's mouth. "I remember when Gage first got interested in Lindsay. That boy drummed up a hundred excuses to drive into town."

"Remember Jeb and Maddy?" Hassie murmured, her eyes flashing with the memory. These were the thoughts she preferred to cling to. Stories with happy resolutions. Good things happening to good people.

Leta's responding grin brightened her face. "I'm not likely to forget. We hadn't seen hide nor hair of him in months."

"Years," Hassie corrected. Following the farming accident that cost Jeb McKenna his leg, the farmer-turned-buffalo-rancher became a recluse. Hassie recalled the days

Joshua had to practically drag his son into town for Christmas dinner. Then Maddy Washburn bought the grocery and started her delivery service. After those two were trapped together in a blizzard, why, there was no counting the number of times Jeb showed up in Buffalo Valley.

"Do you remember the day Margaret Eilers stormed into town and yanked Matt out of Buffalo Bob's?" Leta asked, laughing outright.

"Sure do. She nearly beat him to a pulp." Tears of laughter filled Hassie's eyes. "Can't say I blame her. Those two certainly had their troubles."

Margaret had set her sights on Matt Eilers and wanted him in the worst way, faults and all. That was what she got, too. Not three months after they were married, Margaret found out that Matt had gotten a cocktail waitress pregnant. Granted, it had happened *before* the marriage, but Margaret had still felt angry and betrayed.

"Look at them now," Leta said, sobering. "I don't know any couple more in love." She drank a sip of her tea. "If Margaret and Matt can overcome their problems, why can't Buffalo Valley sort out this thing with Value-X?"

For the first time all week, Hassie felt hopeful. "Maybe you're right, Leta. Maybe you're right."

★ ★ ★

Carrie sat down at the kitchen table and reached for the cream, adding it to her coffee. Even though she was twenty-seven years old, she found it comforting to watch her mother stir up a batch of gingerbread cookies. The house was redolent with the scent of cinnamon and other spices.

Her morning had been busy. After a lengthy conversation with Lindsay Sinclair, who'd been in contact with the Value-X corporate offices, Carrie had spent an hour on the Internet learning what she could about the big retailer.

"Did you have a good time yesterday afternoon?" Diane Hendrickson asked. She set the mixing bowl in the refrigerator, then joined Carrie at the table.

"I had a *wonderful* time." She was surprised to realize how much she meant that. Lowering her eyes momentarily, she looked back up. "I told Vaughn about Alec."

Her mother held her gaze. Carrie didn't often speak of her failed marriage, especially not to new acquaintances.

"It came up naturally, and for the first time I didn't feel that terrible sense of . . . of defeat. I don't think I'll ever be the same person again, but after talking to Vaughn, I knew I don't want to be."

Her mother smiled softly. "There was nothing wrong with you, Carrie."

"That's true, Mom, but I was at fault, too. I suspected Alec was involved with someone else. I simply preferred not to *face* it. The evidence was right in front of my eyes months before he told me. I don't ever again want to be the kind of woman who ignores the truth."

"You've never —"

"Oh, Mom," she said, loving her mother all the more for her unwavering loyalty. "It's time to move forward."

"With Vaughn Kyle?"

Carrie had thought of little else in the past three days. "Too soon to tell."

"But you like him?" her mother pressed.

She nodded. "I do." It felt good to admit it. Good to think that her life wouldn't be forever weighed down by a mistake she'd made when she was too young to understand that her marriage was doomed. Her husband's betrayal had blindsided her. Outwardly she'd picked up the pieces of her shattered pride and continued her life, but in her heart, Carrie had never completely recovered. Alec had shattered her self-esteem. Somehow she'd convinced herself that there must've been something lacking in *her;* it'd taken her a long time to realize the lack had been his.

Carrie drank the rest of her coffee and placed the cup in the sink. "We spoke about Value-X, too, Vaughn and I. At first he didn't seem to see how a company like that would hurt Buffalo Valley. In fact, he felt it might even have a positive effect. If so, I don't see one. But he let me vent my frustrations and helped me clarify my thinking."

"Will you be seeing him again?" her mother asked innocently enough.

"Most likely. He's bringing his mother into town this morning. He's buying her one of Sarah's quilts for Christmas and thought she'd like to choose it herself."

"What a thoughtful gift."

Carrie didn't mention that she'd been the one to suggest it. "They're meeting Hassie later." They hadn't made any definite plans, but Carrie hoped to meet Vaughn's mother. She was almost sure he'd stop by, either here or at the store; in fact, she was counting on it.

The doorbell chimed right then, and fingers crossed, Carrie decided it had to be Vaughn. Her mother went to answer the door.

"Carrie," she called from the living room, "you have a visitor."

"I hope you don't mind me dropping by unexpectedly," he was saying to her mother when Carrie walked in. Vaughn stood awkwardly near the door. He removed his gloves and stuffed them in his pockets.

"Hello, Vaughn." Carrie didn't bother to disguise her pleasure at seeing him again.

"Hi." He looked directly into her eyes. "Would you be free to meet my mother? I left her a few moments ago, drooling over Sarah's quilts."

"I'd like that." Carrie reached into the hall closet for her coat and scarf. "What did you think of the quilts?" she asked, buttoning her coat. She wanted him to appreciate Sarah's talent.

"They're incredible. You're right, it's the perfect gift for Mom."

Carrie supposed she had no business feeling proud; the quilt shop wasn't hers and she had nothing to do with it. But everyone in Buffalo Valley took pride in Sarah's accomplishments. It was more than the fact that Sarah had started the company in her father's living room. People viewed her success as a reflection of what had happened to the town itself — the gradual change from obscurity and scant survival to prosperity and acclaim. Her struggles were their own, and by the same token, her successes were a reason to celebrate.

"I wanted you to know how much I enjoyed our time together yesterday," Vaughn said, matching his steps to hers as they took a shortcut through the park. "I appreciate the suggestion about the quilt. And I learned a lot about you — and Buffalo Valley. You helped me see the town in an entirely different way."

"I was grateful you let me talk out my feelings about Value-X . . . and everything else."

Vaughn's arm came around her and he briefly squeezed her shoulder. There was no need to refer to the divorce. He understood what she meant.

"I talked to Lindsay Sinclair earlier," Carrie said, changing the subject. "She phoned the corporate office and asked if the rumors are true."

"I thought you said they were negotiating for property."

"That's what I told Lindsay, but she doesn't trust Ambrose Kohn. She said she wouldn't put it past him to let people *think* Value-X was interested in the property so Heath or someone else would leap forward and offer to buy it. He's not exactly the kind of person to generate a lot of trust."

"What did your friend find out when she talked to the corporate people?"

"First they said they didn't want to comment on their plans, but when Lindsay pressed the spokeswoman, she admitted that Buffalo Valley's definitely under consideration." Carrie's shoulders tensed. "Lindsay took the opportunity to let her know they aren't welcome in Buffalo Valley." When she'd heard about that part of the conversation, Carrie had cheered.

"What did the company spokeswoman say then?"

Carrie laughed. "Apparently Value-X's official response is that according to their studies, a growing community such as Buffalo Valley doesn't have enough retail choices."

Vaughn snorted.

"That's what I thought. They're sending a representative after Christmas. This person is supposed to win us over and show us everything Value-X can do for Buffalo Valley." She couldn't keep the sarcasm out of her voice.

"It wouldn't hurt to listen," he said mildly.

Carrie whirled on him. "We'll listen, but having a huge chain store in town is *not* what we want. Joanie Wyatt's already started a petition, so when the company representative arrives, he or she will be met with the signature of every single person in town."

Vaughn said nothing.

"What Value-X doesn't understand is that Buffalo Valley is a small town with small-town values and that's exactly the way we want to keep it. If they move in, they'll ruin everything that makes us who we are."

Vaughn stopped in front of a picnic bench, cleared away the snow with his arm and sat down. "What about jobs? Value-X will offer a lot of opportunity to young people. I've heard repeatedly that farming communities are seeing their young adults move away because of the lack of financial security."

"That's not necessarily true, the part about

Value-X bringing jobs. After I talked to Lindsay, I got on the Internet and did some research myself. I learned that most of the positions Value-X brings into a town are part-time and low-paying. They offer few benefits to their employees. The worst aspect is that they destroy more jobs than they create."

Vaughn's frown deepened.

"I apologize," she said. "I didn't mean to get carried away about our problems with Value-X."

Standing, Vaughn still seemed deep in thought. "No, I want to hear this. It bothers me that the company isn't listening to your concerns."

"They don't *want* to listen."

"But you said they're sending a representative."

"Right," she said with a snicker. "To talk to us, not to listen. They're under the mistaken impression that we'll be swayed by a few promises and slick words. They've decided we need to think bigger and bolder and stop acting like a small town."

"But Buffalo Valley *is* a small town."

Carrie gave a sharp nod. "Exactly."

As they approached the Buffalo Valley Quilting Company, Carrie noticed the middle-aged woman standing inside by the window, looking out into the street. When Vaughn and Carrie appeared, she smiled and waved, then pointed to the quilt on display.

Carrie waved back, silently applauding his mother's choice.

Mrs. Kyle smiled. Her eyes moved to her son and then to Carrie; her expression grew quizzical. Carrie didn't have time to guess what that meant before Mrs. Kyle opened the glass door, stepped out and introduced herself.

Barbara Kyle knew that when she agreed to accompany Vaughn into Buffalo Valley, she'd be seeing Hassie Knight. A meeting was inevitable. They hadn't been together since the day they'd stood in the pouring rain as a military casket was lowered into the ground.

Following the funeral, she'd kept in touch with Vaughn's mother. They'd called each other frequently. But despite the war, despite her grief, Barbara's college courses had continued, and she'd had to immerse herself in a very different kind of reality.

Rick had lost his best friend, and they began to seek solace from each other. Falling in love with him was a surprise. Barbara hadn't expected that, hadn't thought it was possible to love again after losing Vaughn. Rick wasn't a replacement. No one could ever replace the man she'd loved. He understood, because in his own way he'd loved Vaughn, too.

When they announced their engagement,

Hassie had pulled away from Barbara. Neither spoke of it, but they both knew that their relationship had fundamentally changed and that their former closeness could no longer exist. Vaughn's parents didn't attend the wedding, although they'd mailed a card and sent a generous check.

Barbara thought now that naming their son after Vaughn Knight had as much to do with Hassie as it did with their feelings for Vaughn. Perhaps she'd hoped to bridge the distance between them. . . .

Until he was twenty-one, Hassie had remembered Vaughn Kyle every year on his birthday, but that was the only time Barbara and Rick heard from her. When Rick accepted early retirement and they'd decided to move back to North Dakota, Barbara recognized that, sooner or later, she'd see Hassie again. A month or so after they'd moved, Hassie had welcomed them with a brief note. It seemed fitting that Barbara's son had been the one to arrange this meeting, to bring them together again.

"Hassie wanted me to bring you to the house, instead of the pharmacy," Vaughn said as they left the quilting store.

"You're coming with us, aren't you?" Barbara asked Carrie. She'd quickly grasped that Vaughn was attracted to this woman, and she could understand why. However, she didn't pretend to know what was happening.

Natalie had phoned several times, wanting to speak to Vaughn; she wasn't amused that he'd apparently turned off his cell phone. Barbara didn't feel it was her place to inform the other woman that Vaughn was out with someone else. The situation concerned her, but she couldn't interfere and had to trust that he was treating both women with honesty and fairness.

"I'd love to come to Hassie's with you," Carrie told them, "but I said I'd fill in at the store for her. You two go and have a good visit, and I'll see you later."

As they crossed the street, Carrie headed toward the pharmacy, and Barbara and Vaughn went in the opposite direction.

"Does the pharmacy still have the soda fountain?" Barbara asked her son.

"Sure does. In fact, I thought I'd leave you and Hassie to visit, and I'd steal away to Knight's to let Carrie fix me a soda."

"You're spending a lot of time with her, aren't you?" Barbara couldn't resist asking.

"Am I?"

Barbara didn't answer him. There was probably some perfect maternal response, but darned if she knew what it was.

Hassie's house came into view, and Barbara automatically slowed her pace. It'd been thirty-three years since she'd walked up these steps. Thirty-three years since she'd attended the wake, sat in a corner of the living room with Vaughn's older sister and wept bitter tears. At the end of a day that had been too long for all of them, Vaughn's mother had hugged her close and then instructed a family friend to make sure Barbara got safely home to Grand Forks.

"Mom?" Vaughn studied her and seemed to sense that something was wrong.

"It's all right," she said. Funny how quickly those old emotions resurfaced. Her stomach churned as if it'd been only a few months since she'd last walked this path. But thirty-three years, a lifetime, had passed.

Hassie opened the door before Barbara could ring the bell. They stood there for a moment, gazing into each other's eyes.

Hassie smiled then, a welcoming smile that seemed to reach deep inside her with its warmth and generosity. "Barbara," the older woman said, flinging open the screen door.

When she'd entered the house, Hassie hugged her for long minutes, and Barbara felt the tears gather in her eyes.

"I'm so glad you came." Hassie finally released her and embraced Vaughn, who stood quietly behind his mother. "I assume Vaughn told you about our visit?"

"Yes, he did. I can't tell you how honored we all are that you'd give him Mr. Knight's gold watch."

"It seemed right that he have it." She took Barbara's coat and hung it in the hall closet.

"I won't take yours," she said to Vaughn, her back to them both. "You're probably planning to sneak over to the shop for a soda."

"How'd you guess?"

"I was young once myself," Hassie said, and shooed him out the door.

"Carrie's a wonderful young woman," Hassie told her as soon as Vaughn had left.

"They certainly seem to have taken a liking to one another," Barbara said noncommittally. She liked what she'd seen of Carrie — but what about Natalie? Well, that was Vaughn's business, she reminded herself again.

Hassie led her into the living room. "I hope you don't mind, but I've already poured the tea."

"Not at all."

The silver service was set up on the coffee table and two delicate china cups were neatly positioned, steam rising from the recently poured tea. A plate of cookies had been placed nearby.

"I don't often get an excuse to use my good tea service and china these days," Hassie murmured.

The two women sat side by side on the dark-blue sofa and sipped their tea. Neither really knew where to start, Barbara reflected. She took a deep breath.

"I've thought of you often," she said. "Especially since you were so generous with our son."

"He must have thought me a silly old woman, writing him little tidbits of advice."

"Hassie," Barbara said, and touched Hassie's forearm. "*No one* could think that." She shook her head. "He saved every birthday card you ever sent him. And he remembered what you wrote. He grew up honorable and generous, and I can't help thinking you played a part in that."

Hassie smiled her appreciation. "Nonsense, but it's very kind of you to say so."

Barbara glanced around the room. "Being here brings back so many memories," she said. The house, this room, was exactly as she remembered. She suspected that even after all these years, Vaughn's bedroom was virtually untouched. She remembered the high-school banner he had pinned to the wall and the bedroom set, old-fashioned even then. Valerie's old room was probably the same as it had been, as well, just like the rest of this house.

Hassie didn't comment, and Barbara sensed that the older woman had hung on to the past as much as she could and found comfort in what was familiar. Hassie's strength was considerable, but her loss had been too great. *Losses,* Barbara recalled. Jerry had died not long afterward, and Valerie had moved to Hawaii.

"Do you like living in Grand Forks?"

Hassie asked, turning away from reminders of grief.

"Very much. My parents leased out the house when they moved to Arizona. Rick and I always intended to move here one day, and I'm really happy we did. This will be our first Christmas in North Dakota since Vaughn was five or six."

"With family again."

"Actually, there'll only be Rick, Vaughn and me. All my family has moved away, and Gloria, our daughter, lives in Dallas."

"Have Christmas here with me," Hassie urged, and then as if she regretted the impulse, she shook her head. "No, please forget I asked. I'm sorry to impose. It's just the rambling of an old woman."

"Hassie, if you're serious, we'd love nothing better than to spend the day with you."

Hassie's eyes shone. "You mean you'd actually consider coming?"

"We'd be honored. I know Rick would love to see you again. He wanted to join me today, but he was already committed to something else — some volunteer work he's doing."

"You're sure about Christmas?"

"Very sure," Barbara insisted. "But I can't allow you to do all the cooking."

"Oh," Hassie said, "it's no problem. I'd enjoy preparing my favorite recipes."

"We'll share the meal preparation, then,"

Barbara compromised, and Hassie agreed.

"We'll be having Christmas dinner," Barbara murmured, "with a dear, dear friend."

"I can't think of anything I'd enjoy more."

Barbara couldn't, either.

Chapter 5

Carrie found Leta tending Knight's Pharmacy when she arrived after saying goodbye to Vaughn and his mother.

"Thanks for filling in for me," she said, hurrying to the back of the store. She stored her coat and purse and pulled on her white jacket.

"I don't mind staying," Leta told her. "In fact, Hassie asked me if I would. She thought you and Vaughn might like a few hours together." Leta wiped down the counter, and Carrie noticed how the other woman's eyes managed to evade hers.

"Aren't you two being just a little obvious?" she teased.

"Perhaps," Leta said, "but we both think it's high time you got into circulation again."

"Like a library book?" Carrie said with a grin. "I've been on the shelf too long?"

"Laugh if you want, but it's true. You've been avoiding a social life. That's not good for a woman of your age."

Carrie was about to explain that, while she appreciated their efforts, she'd already spent time with Vaughn. Before she could, though, the bell above the door chimed, and Lindsay Sinclair and her two daughters stepped into the warmth of the pharmacy.

"Grandma." Four-year-old Joy ran toward Leta, who scooped the girl up in her arms for an enthusiastic hug.

"I've had the most incredible morning," Lindsay announced.

"Value-X?" Carrie asked.

Lindsay nodded. "The spokeswoman actually phoned me back."

"She called you?" Leta asked, voice incredulous, as she set Joy back on the floor.

"Yes, and for some reason, she seemed to view me as a contact who represented the community. That's fine, since everyone in town shares my opinion." Lindsay removed her hat and shook out her hair. "She wanted me to understand that Value-X intends to be a good neighbor, quote, unquote."

"Yeah, right!" Carrie muttered sarcastically.

"I'll just bet," Leta added. "They assume we're nothing but a bunch of dumb hicks."

"To be fair," Lindsay said, glancing between the other two women, "we don't know *what* they think of us — not that we have any interest in their opinion. But we are fully capable of mounting a campaign to keep them out."

"I was thinking the same thing," Carrie said.

"Organization is the key," Leta put in.

"You'll be at the Cookie Exchange tonight, won't you?" Lindsay asked Carrie. "I know Leta will." She smiled at her mother-in-law. "I thought that would be the best time to get all the women together. We can talk then."

"Good idea. Mom and I will be there for sure." The women's group at the church held the cookie exchange every Christmas. Joyce Dawson, the pastor's wife, had been instrumental in organizing the event, and every woman in town and the surrounding community could be counted on to attend.

"Value-X won't know what hit them," Leta said happily.

The bell chimed a second time, and Vaughn entered the store. For a moment, he seemed startled to see the three women, but then his gaze sought out Carrie's. "Should I come back later?"

"Not at all," Leta said. "There's no need for Carrie to work today. I've got everything covered."

Carrie was grateful for what her friends were trying to do, but she did have responsibilities. Leta seemed to read her thoughts. "If any prescriptions get phoned in, I'll find you," she promised. "I'll leave a message with your mom."

"Ever hear the expression about not looking a gift horse in the mouth?" Lindsay whispered.

"Well, it appears I'm not wanted or needed

around here," Carrie said before Leta and Hassie's intentions became any plainer than they already were. She walked past Lindsay, who winked at her. After collecting her coat and purse, Carrie left with Vaughn.

"Where would you like to go?" he asked as soon as they were outside.

She hadn't had lunch yet and suspected Vaughn hadn't, either. "I know we had Italian yesterday, but I love pizza."

"Me, too."

"Buffalo Valley has some of the best home-made pizza you'll ever eat."

He lifted his eyebrows. "Sounds good to me."

They started down the street, their pace relaxed. Snow had just begun to fall, drifting earthward in large, soft flakes. Christmas-card snow, Carrie thought. As they walked, she told him the story about Rachel's pizza, and how it had led to her restaurant and subsequent success.

"You mean she makes the sauce herself?"

Carrie nodded. "I worked for Rachel one summer and I watched her make a batch. She starts with fresh tomatoes straight from her garden. It's amazingly good. I think she could sell her recipe, but of course, she doesn't want to."

A pickup approached and slowed as it came alongside Vaughn and Carrie. Glancing over her shoulder, Carrie saw her two older brothers, Tom and Pete. She tried to ignore them, but that was impossible.

"Hey, Carrie," Tom called, leaning his elbow out the open passenger window.

She acknowledged his greeting with a short wave, hoping he'd simply move on. Not that this was likely. Apparently Chuck and Ken had mentioned Vaughn, and now they, too, were looking for an introduction.

"Don't you want us to meet your friend?"

"Not right now," she called back, and sent Vaughn an apologetic glance. Because she was the only girl, all four of her brothers were protective of her, even more so after her divorce.

"You ashamed of your family?" This came from Pete, who was driving.

Carrie sighed, praying that her brothers wouldn't say or do anything to further embarrass her. Pete parked the truck and both men climbed out, slamming their doors extra hard. Both wore thick winter coats and wool caps with the earflaps dangling. They were large men and did their best to appear intimidating.

She made the introductions, gesturing weakly toward her brothers. Vaughn stepped forward and shook hands with both of them.

"Nice to finally meet you," Tom said, resting his foot on the truck's bumper. "Now I'd like to know what your intentions are toward my sister."

"Tom!" Furious, Carrie clenched her fists. "This is *none* of your business."

"The day you stop being my sister is the day I stop caring who you date."

"Well . . ." Vaughn clearly had no idea what to say.

Her brothers putting him on the spot like this was outrageous. Picking up a handful of snow, Carrie immediately formed a ball and threw it at her oldest brother, hitting him square in the chest. Not waiting for his reaction, Carrie grabbed Vaughn's arm and shouted, "Run!"

"You asked for this, Carrie Ann," Tom shouted as Carrie and Vaughn raced across the street. They had just entered the park when Carrie felt her backside pelted by two snowballs.

"This is war," Vaughn yelled when he saw that she'd been hit. He leaned down and packed his own snow, then hurled two balls in quick succession, hitting both Pete and Tom. Her brothers reacted with stunned surprise.

Laughing and dodging around the play equipment with her brothers in hot pursuit, Carrie had trouble keeping pace with Vaughn. He yelled instructions and pointed toward the back of Hamburger Heaven. The stand was closed for the winter and offered ample protection, but a few moments later, her brothers found them and began to bombard them with a flurry of snowballs. Although most of them hit the side of the building, it was obvious that Vaughn and Carrie couldn't stay there long.

"You ready to surrender yet?" Pete demanded.

"Never," Vaughn answered for them.

"This way," Carrie told him. With the community Christmas tree blocking their movements, she led him across the street. Hidden by a loaded hay truck that passed behind them, Carrie steered him toward her parents' store.

"This is what I'd consider enemy territory," Vaughn whispered as they slipped behind the building and out of view.

"But it's the last place they'll look," she assured him.

"Smart thinking." Vaughn beamed her a delighted smile.

She smiled back — and realized she hadn't felt this kind of pure, uninhibited pleasure in . . . years. Since childhood, probably. When she didn't break eye contact and started to laugh, he said, "What?"

She shook her head, not wanting to put into words the joy she felt.

A sound startled them both, and they froze. Carrie was certain her brothers had found them again, but if it *was* Pete and Tom, they left without searching farther.

Relieved, Carrie sighed and slumped

against the wall. "I believe we're safe for the moment. Are you still interested in that pizza?"

Vaughn nodded, but she saw a strange expression in his eyes as he continued to gaze down at her. Carrie tried to look away and couldn't. She knew he intended to kiss her, and she shut her eyes as he moved closer. She'd been waiting for this moment, anticipating it. Wrapping her arms around his neck, she leaned into him. He drew off his gloves and then her wool hat and dropped them. Weaving his hands into her hair, he kissed her . . . and deepened the kiss until they were both breathless. Carrie trembled and buried her face in his shoulder. Neither spoke. As he held her tight, it seemed for those few moments that their hearts beat in unison.

He kissed her again, his mouth both firm and soft. When he eased away, Carried noticed that his brow had furrowed, and she thought she read doubt in his eyes. Uncertainty. She touched his face, wondering at the confusion she saw in him. "Is anything wrong?" she asked.

He answered with a quick shake of his head. "Everything is right."

And yet he sounded reluctant. She wanted to ask him more, but he moved away from her and peeked around the back wall. "Do you think it's safe now?" he asked.

"It should be. Pete and Tom were just having fun with us."

"Protective older brothers."

"Exactly."

"I watched over Gloria, too," he said. "She's two years younger than me."

"Just imagine that four times over."

"I don't need to," Vaughn said, ostentatiously brushing evidence of the snow battle from his sleeves.

They didn't see Pete or Tom on their way over, so Carrie assumed they'd gone about their business. As she'd told Vaughn, it'd been all in fun and at least her brothers knew when to admit defeat.

Predictably enough, Vaughn raved about the pizza. In fact, he bought a second one to take home and reheat. When they'd eaten, they returned to Hassie's, where his mother had just finished her visit. All four of them walked to where Vaughn had parked the car outside Sarah's quilt store. When they reached it, Hassie and Barbara Kyle hugged for a long moment.

"Thank you for coming," Hassie said, dabbing at her eyes.

Carrie knew it had been an emotional visit for both women.

"No — thank *you* for . . . for being Hassie," Barbara said, and they hugged again. "I'll be in touch about Christmas."

Vaughn opened the car door for his mother

and helped her inside, an old-fashioned courtesy that reminded Carrie of her father and uncles.

Carrie stood on the sidewalk next to Hassie as Vaughn placed his pizza carefully on the back seat.

"They're coming to spend Christmas with me," Hassie said. "I haven't looked forward to anything so much in years. It'll be like when the children were still home."

Carrie knew Hassie intended to spend Christmas morning with Bob and Merrily and little Bobby, but she'd turned down invitations from almost everyone in town for dinner. Carrie was relieved that Hassie wouldn't spend the afternoon alone — and she envied her Vaughn's company.

He climbed into the car beside his mother and started the engine. Before he backed out of the parking space, his eyes met Carrie's. She raised her hand and he returned the gesture. She felt as if her heart was reaching out to him . . . and his to her.

Chapter 6

Hassie had been looking forward to this night. The Dawsons had moved to Buffalo Valley four years earlier; at that time the only church in town had been Catholic and was closed after Father McGrath's retirement. Then Reverend John Dawson and his wife had arrived.

What a blessing the couple had turned out to be! Joyce knew instinctively what to say to make people feel welcome. John's sermons were inspiring, and his advice was both sensitive and practical.

Her first Christmas in Buffalo Valley, Joyce had organized the Cookie Exchange, which had become a yearly event.

Hassie had baked oatmeal-cranberry cookies early that morning and set out a plate for her visit with Barbara. Both had gotten so involved in their conversation that they hadn't tasted a single one. Hassie shook her head, smiling. It was as though all those years of not seeing each other had simply vanished after their initial awkwardness had passed. The visit had gone by far too quickly; Barbara had to leave long before Hassie was ready. What amazed Hassie was that she'd found herself saying things she hadn't even realized she felt.

Her daughter's decision to live in Hawaii was one example. She'd never understood what had prompted Valerie's choice. Yes, there'd been a job offer, but Valerie had *pursued* that job. The fact was, she'd wanted to get as far away from North Dakota as she possibly could. Hassie understood this for the very first time.

When Barbara had inquired about Valerie, Hassie explained that her daughter had chosen to remove herself from the pain of losing her only brother and then her father. Never before had Hassie consciously acknowledged that. Yet the moment she said the words, she knew they were true.

Later that evening when Hassie got to the church for the Cookie Exchange, the place was blazing with light. Although she was twenty minutes early, the parking lot was already half-full. The first person she saw once she'd set her platter of cookies on the table was Calla Stern. Sarah's once-rebellious daughter had become a lovely young woman. She was in her junior year of college now, if Hassie recalled correctly, and there was talk of her applying for admission to law school. She attended the University of Chicago and shared an apartment nearby, but at heart Calla remained a small-town girl.

As soon as Calla saw Hassie, she broke off her conversation and hurried across the room, arms outstretched.

"When did you get home?" Hassie asked, hugging her close.

"This afternoon. Oh, Hassie, I just heard about Value-X. What are we going to do?"

"I don't know, Calla, and this might shock you all, but I've decided I'm too old to fight them."

Calla frowned.

"That's what Leta told us."

"We can't stand in the way of progress." *If progress it is.* Change, anyway. Perhaps if Hassie repeated that often enough, she might come to accept it. This wasn't what she wanted, but as she'd learned long ago, the world didn't revolve around what she assumed was best.

"Let's enjoy this evening," Hassie urged, "and put these worries behind us until the new year."

"I'll try," the girl promised.

"Good." Hassie slid her arm through Calla's. "Now tell me, are you still seeing Kevin?" Calla had been dating Leta's boy off and on since her last year of high school.

"Occasionally. He's so busy, and I'm in school most of the time. Anyway, with him in Paris for six months . . ."

"Calla would make a wonderful daughter-in-law," Leta said, joining them.

"Oh, you!" Calla hugged her tightly, laughing as Hassie seconded Leta's remark.

"Stop it, you two," the girl chided. "I'm dating someone else at the moment and so is Kevin. We're good friends, but that's all. For now, anyway."

"Damn," Leta muttered.

"Give them time," Hassie told her.

"Exactly," Calla said with a soft smile, and after kissing them both, added, "Now excuse me while I go mingle."

Hassie watched her leave. She thought Calla and Kevin would eventually get married, but probably not for some years. Not until educations were completed and careers launched. Still, they understood each other and shared the experience of having grown up in Buffalo Valley.

No sooner had Calla wandered off than Maddy appeared with four-year-old Julianne. She was heavily pregnant with her third child, but she'd lost none of her composure or contentment.

"Maddy," Hassie said, pleased to see her. "Here, let me help you with all that." Maddy was juggling her coat and purse, plus a huge box of homemade cookies.

"Mommy, can I play with Joy?" Julianne asked, tugging at Maddy's sleeve.

"Yes, sweetheart, and tell Lindsay I'll be right there."

"Where's little Caleb?" Hassie asked.

"With his daddy. After all, this is a *girls'* night out," Maddy said. Hassie knew this third pregnancy was as unexpected as their first. With three babies in five years, Jeb and Maddy were sure to have their hands full for quite a while.

Jeb's mother must be looking down from heaven, mighty pleased with her son, Hassie mused. Thanks to Maddy, he'd gone from curmudgeonly recluse to good husband and proud father.

Hassie and Leta busied themselves arranging platters of cookies on the long tables. Joyce made several trips to the business office to run recipes off on the copier so they'd be available for whoever wanted them.

Margaret Eilers and her daughter, Hailey, were among the last to arrive. Hailey, at three, bore a strong resemblance to her father and to her brother, David. Looking at Margaret and the child, no one would guess she wasn't the girl's birth mother. Hassie had nothing but praise for the way Matt and Margaret had worked out the awkward situation involving their children.

In the beginning Hassie hadn't been keen on Matt Eilers. No one in town held a high opinion of the rancher. But Margaret had fallen hard for Matt; she wanted to marry him and nothing would change her mind. After Bernard died and left her the ranch, Matt started seeing more and more of her. A few months later, there was a wedding. Then, lo and behold, Margaret turned up pregnant — at the same time as that woman in Devils Lake.

The babies were born within a few weeks of each other, Hailey first and then little David. Hailey had been living with the couple for most of her three years. She was a darling little girl, which Hassie attributed primarily to the love and attention Margaret lavished on her.

The room rang with laughter and cheer, and Hassie basked in the sounds that ebbed and flowed around her. Her day had started early and been an emotional one. When she noticed chairs arranged along the wall, she slipped quietly off and sat down. A few minutes later Leta came to sit beside her.

"Just listen," Hassie said, closing her eyes.

"What am I supposed to be listening to?" Leta asked.

"The joy," Hassie told her. "The friendship. These women are the very breath of this community." Hassie was grateful she'd lived long enough to witness the town's reversal of fortunes. It was because of women like Lindsay and Rachel and Maddy and Sarah and Joanie Wyatt. . . . And maybe she herself had played a small part.

"What I can't get over is all the babies," Leta said. "Future generations for Buffalo Valley."

"Rachel Quantrill is pregnant again," Hassie said, nodding at the young woman on the other side of the room talking with Sarah. Hassie was particularly fond of Rachel. She'd watched the young widow struggle to get by after the death of her first husband. She'd driven a school bus and worked as a part-time bookkeeper for Hassie. Later she'd opened the pizza-delivery service. That was how she'd met Heath. New to the banking business, Heath had rejected her loan application. His grandmother, who'd started the bank, had been furious with him, Hassie recalled. But things had a way of working out for the best. Lily Quantrill had lived to see her grandson and Rachel marry. Rachel had brought a son into the marriage, and later she and Heath had a daughter they'd named after Lily. A third child was expected in early summer.

"I'll have to remember that," Hassie murmured absently.

Leta gave her a puzzled look. "What?"

Hassie wasn't aware she'd spoken aloud. "About things working out for the best." Despite her efforts, her thoughts had returned to Value-X and the potential for disaster. All her hopes for this town and the people she loved so dearly were at stake.

"You feeling all right?" Leta asked in a concerned tone.

"I'm fine," Hassie assured her. "Just tired. It's been a busy day."

Joyce Dawson sat down at the piano, and soon the room was filled with sweetly raised voices. The women and children gathered around, breaking naturally into two-part harmony. To Hassie it sounded as though the very angels from heaven were singing.

"Hassie —" Carrie Hendrickson crouched by her chair "— are you ill?"

Leta answered for her. "She's just tired."

"No wonder," Carrie murmured. "She was up before dawn baking cookies and then there was the visit from Barbara Kyle, plus a big order came in for the pharmacy."

Hassie grinned, amused that they spoke as if she wasn't even there.

"Let me walk you home," Carrie suggested, taking her hand.

"Fiddlesticks. I'm perfectly capable of walking back on my own. No need for you to leave the party."

"I insist," Carrie said. "It'll only take a few minutes and no one will miss me."

Hassie was weary, wearier than she cared to admit, so she agreed. Carrie retrieved their coats and led the way outside, sliding her arm through Hassie's to lend her support. They walked slowly, in companionable silence. The night sky was bright and clear, the stars scattered against it like diamonds. Most of the snow had been swept aside and the sidewalks salted.

As they crossed the street, a truck pulled

up to the curb and rolled down the window. "You two need a ride?" Chuck Hendrickson asked.

"We're fine, thanks, anyway," Carrie told her brother.

"Say, that fellow you had dinner with phoned a few minutes ago."

"Must be Vaughn," Hassie said. It did seem that Carrie and Vaughn were seeing a lot of each other, and that pleased her. From now on, Hassie resolved to look only at the positive side of things. She refused to let herself fret over situations she couldn't control.

"I'll call him back once I'm finished over at the church," Carrie told her brother, who drove off.

"You could do worse, Carrie," Hassie said. "He's a fine man."

"I think so, too."

"Not every man is another Alec."

"I know," she said.

Hassie patted Carrie's hand. She would go home and think good thoughts for the young woman and for Buffalo Valley. Happy, positive thoughts.

"It's about time you called," Natalie snapped. There'd been no word of greeting.

Vaughn sat on the bed in his parents' guest room and pressed his cell phone to his ear. He felt guilty about not returning Natalie's repeated calls. He'd delayed it, needing to

131

put his thoughts in order first. He felt guilty about other things, too, but he didn't want to think about Carrie, not when he had to deal with Natalie.

No one in Buffalo Valley knew he'd taken a job with Value-X. Not his parents. Not Hassie. And certainly not Carrie. His visit to North Dakota at a time when the company was considering an outlet in this area had seemed a fortuitous coincidence. Now it felt like the very opposite. He'd agreed to check out the town, but that had been a mistake he regretted heartily. And Natalie was hounding him for information.

"You're right, I should've phoned sooner," he admitted.

"Yes, you should have." Her voice softened. "I've missed hearing from you."

He didn't have an excuse to offer her, and the truth was . . . well, difficult to explain. Not only did he have serious doubts about working for this company, he'd met Carrie, and the attraction between them was undeniable.

Just a few days ago his future had seemed assured, but now, after meeting Hassie and Carrie, his entire sense of what was right had been challenged. And his assumptions about love and marriage, about Natalie — they'd changed, too.

Natalie's voice was hard when she spoke again. "I was beginning to wonder if I made a mistake recommending you for this position. I put my reputation on the line."

"I assumed I'd been hired on my own merits."

"You were but . . ." She sighed heavily. "Let's forget all that, shall we? I didn't know what to think when you didn't phone." She gave a stilted laugh. "I realize you're not officially on the payroll until January, but it's so advantageous for you to be near this little town."

"The town has a name."

"I know that," she said, and some of the stiffness returned to her voice. "I'm sorry, Vaughn, but I've had a trying day. Apparently Buffalo Valley is mounting opposition against Value-X."

"I know."

"You do?" She slowly released her breath. "You can't imagine how hectic everything is here, with the holidays and everything else. Now *this*. I spoke with a woman in town. I can't remember her name exactly. Lesley, Lindy . . ."

"Lindsay Sinclair."

"You know her?"

"I've met her."

"She made the town's position very clear," Natalie continued. "It seems we've got some public-relations work ahead of us. Okay, we can deal with that — we've done it before. We know how to present our case in a positive light. It won't take much to change their attitude, and really, at this point, they really don't have much choice."

Vaughn was sorry to hear that. So it was too late; Value-X had obviously succeeded in buying the property. This was what he'd feared. "Lindsay told me Value-X is sending someone out after Christmas."

"I volunteered for the job myself," she said, excited now. "It was providential, don't you think? I can meet your parents and settle this unfortunate matter with Buffalo Valley at the same time. Combine business with pleasure, in other words." She sounded pleased with herself for having so neatly arranged this trip. "I've got everything in motion for a Value-X campaign."

"I hope you'll be willing to listen to the town's concerns."

"Well, yes, of course I'll listen, but I'm hoping to present our case, too. In fact, I've already authorized a letter to be delivered to every family in Buffalo Valley. It's scheduled to arrive just after the first of the year."

"A letter?"

"Everyone thinks it's a great idea." Her satisfaction was unmistakable. "I wrote it myself for a personal touch. I want the town to understand that they've unfairly prejudged Value-X. I told them not to look at any negatives they might've heard about the company, but at the positives — everything we can do for their community. We plan to be a good neighbor."

Vaughn knew that Natalie's letter would most likely anger the people of Buffalo Valley, not reassure them. "I didn't realize you'd signed the deal on the land," he muttered. Without being completely aware of it, Vaughn had held out hope that the controversy would die a natural death if the land deal fell through. His heart sank. It looked as if he'd have no choice now but to get involved. The question was: on which side would he stand? If he followed his heart, he'd join Hassie and Carrie in their fight, but if he did that, he'd compromise his future with Value-X and Natalie . . .

Natalie hesitated before she answered. "There've been a few snags with the property deal. Mr. Kohn isn't an easy man to work with."

Vaughn's relief was swift. So there *was* hope. "That's what I hear about Ambrose Kohn."

"Have you met him?"

"No, he lives in Devils Lake. Listen, Natalie, I have to tell you I'm not convinced Buffalo Valley is a good site."

She laughed, but he could tell she wasn't amused. "You haven't even started work yet and you're already telling me my job?"

"*You* chose Buffalo Valley as a development site?"

"I sure did," she said smugly. "We did a study on small towns that have shown substantial growth over the last five years. Buffalo Valley is a perfect target area for retail expansion."

Vaughn's hand tightened around the telephone receiver. "They don't have enough retail choices," he muttered.

"Exactly." Apparently she hadn't noticed the sarcasm in his voice.

Vaughn felt tension creeping across his shoulders. He probably couldn't influence her to change her letter or withdraw it; he was in no position to tell Natalie news she didn't want to hear.

She returned to the subject of Ambrose Kohn. "I'm interested in what you know about him," she said.

"I don't know him, but I have heard about him." Vaughn didn't feel comfortable saying anything more than he already had. As it was, he felt traitor enough.

"He *will* sign, and soon." Natalie's confidence sounded unshakable. "The transaction is as good as done."

Vaughn rotated his neck in order to ease the tension.

"I know what's happened," she said, catching him by surprise. "You've seen this little town and now you have doubts that Value-X is doing the right thing."

It was as though she'd read his mind. He found himself nodding.

"You're confused," Natalie continued. "It

happens to a lot of us when we first hire on with the company. Don't worry, it's something we all work through. Trust me, Vaughn, Value-X knows what it's doing."

"Buffalo Valley is afraid of losing its character."

"Every town is in the beginning. They get over it. Sooner or later, each town comes to realize that we know what's best for them. Buffalo Valley will, too."

This was worse than he'd thought. Vaughn rubbed his hand down his face. Still sitting on the edge of his bed, he tilted his head back to stare up at the ceiling. This was *really* bad.

Value-X had no intention of listening to the concerns of Buffalo Valley's citizens. In its arrogance, the retailer had decided on a course of action, one that reflected solely its own interests.

"I'm looking forward to seeing you," Natalie told him, lowering her voice seductively.

It was almost more than Vaughn could do to echo the sentiment.

When he finished the conversation, he returned to the kitchen to find his mother dishing up ice cream.

"You interested?" she asked, holding up the scoop.

"Sure, why not?" he muttered. He took a third bowl from the cupboard and handed it to this mother, who pried open the carton lid.

"Tell me more about Natalie," she said.

Vaughn didn't know what to say. "You'll meet her soon enough."

"She's joining us after Christmas, right?" She studied him hard, and Vaughn knew what she was thinking. He'd spent almost every day of the past week with Carrie. He was with one woman and had another waiting in the wings — that was how it looked. His mother's eyes filled with questions.

"Natalie is coming, then?" she repeated when he didn't answer.

"So it seems." He sighed. She'd show up even if he asked her to stay home. Value-X was paying for the trip.

"You don't sound too happy about it," his mother murmured, her eyes narrowed. "What about Carrie?"

"Mom . . ."

"I know, I know, but I can't help wondering if you're really sure of what you want. I saw the look Carrie gave you as we left Buffalo Valley earlier today."

Vaughn frowned.

"She deserves your honesty."

He was in full agreement; he owed Carrie the truth, and not only about his relationship with Natalie. He had to tell her about Value-X.

As soon as his mother left the kitchen, Vaughn reached for the phone. Unfortunately Carrie wasn't home. He recalled now that she'd mentioned something about meeting with the church women's group, but that'd slipped his mind. He left a message with one of her brothers.

After that, he joined his parents in the living room. He settled on the sofa next to his mother and focused his attention on a television show about Christmas traditions around the world.

An hour later the phone pealed and his mother automatically rose to answer it. She returned almost immediately. "It's Carrie for you."

Vaughn went into the kitchen.

"Hi," she said excitedly when he picked up the receiver. "I just got back from the Cookie Exchange and got your message."

"How was it?"

"Great, as usual. There was a lot of talk about this Value-X problem. We're going to take active measures to keep the company out of town."

She'd given him the perfect lead. This was his chance to explain the whole confused mess. But Vaughn didn't. He couldn't, not over the phone. It was something that needed to be said face-to-face, he decided. Okay, so he was a coward.

Carrie seemed to be waiting for a response,

so to keep the conversation going, he asked, "What can be done?"

"According to Hassie, nothing. She's afraid we can't win, especially after everything she's heard and read. According to all the news stories, the company practically always comes out on top. Still, there are a few towns that didn't give in, including one in Montana, I think." She paused. "Hassie's real problem is that she's just tired out. But I'm not, and neither are the rest of us."

Vaughn could hear the fighting spirit in her voice.

"I suggest you start with Ambrose Kohn." That was probably more than he should've said, but the words escaped before he could judge their wisdom.

"We're having an organizational meeting as soon as it can be arranged, and I'll recommend that."

"Great," he mumbled, wishing he could tell her he didn't want to hear any of this. It put him in a terrible position. He'd be a traitor to Value-X and Natalie if he withheld these facts, and a traitor to Carrie if he relayed them.

". . . tomorrow night."

"I'm sorry," Vaughn said, trapped in his own dilemma. "What did you say?"

"Can you come? It's the high-school play. I know it doesn't sound like much, but we're all proud of it. The play's about the history of Buffalo Valley and the families that settled here. It'll give you a feel for the town."

Vaughn's own great-grandparents on his mother's side had settled in the Dakotas in the late 1800s. He pondered Carrie's words. Knowing more about the town's past might help him decide what to do about his relationship with Value-X — and Natalie. It was a faint hope — and maybe just another delaying tactic — but he had nothing else to cling to.

"Will you come as my guest?" she asked.

"I'll look forward to it."

She gave him the details and Vaughn hung up the phone feeling as vulnerable and unsure as ever.

"How'd it go?" his mother asked when he returned to the living room.

"Fine," he muttered. "Just fine."

Chapter 7

The theater was filled to capacity. People crowded the aisle, chatting and visiting with one another. Carrie had been fortunate to get good seats for herself and Vaughn, thanks to Lindsay Sinclair.

"I didn't know there were this many people in Buffalo Valley," Vaughn said, twisting around to glance over his shoulder.

"There aren't. Folks come from all over. The Cowans drove down from Canada. Her great-grandmother is one of the main characters in the play."

Vaughn looked at his program. "So, Lindsay Sinclair is the producer and director of Dakota Christmas."

Carrie nodded. "Lindsay's the person responsible for all this," she said, gesturing toward her friend. "None of it would've happened without her."

Carrie went on to explain how the play had been created and described everything Lindsay had done to make sure it got performed. At the end of the story she told him that the theater belonged to Ambrose Kohn.

"*The* Ambrose Kohn?" Vaughn's brows arched.

"When Lindsay first arrived, the theater was nothing but cobwebs and dirt. She was a first-year teacher and one of the stipulations when she accepted the job was that the community would pitch in and help."

"In what way?"

"In whatever way she required. She asked the town's older people to talk to the kids. It started with Joshua McKenna. At the time he was president of the town council, plus he knows quite a bit of local history. After that, Lindsay lined up community representatives to come to the school on Friday afternoons. Joshua was the one who gave her the idea of having the kids write the play."

"The high-schoolers wrote the play?"

"The original script was created by the kids Lindsay taught six years ago. Each new group of students refines it a little bit."

"This is the sixth year?" He glanced around with what appeared to be renewed appreciation. "Pretty impressive audience."

"It's a fabulous play. Why else would so many people return year after year?"

"What's your favorite part?"

"I love all of it. There's a scene early on when a tornado hits the town and everything's destroyed. The people lose heart. Entire crops are wiped out and families are left homeless. You can just *feel* their agony." She didn't mean to get carried away, but no matter how often she'd seen it, the scene brought tears to Carrie's eyes.

"What happens then?" Vaughn asked.

"Everyone pulls together. The people whose fields were spared share their crops with the ones who lost everything. With everyone working together, they rebuild the farms destroyed in the tornado and save the town."

Vaughn nodded slowly. "Teamwork," he murmured.

"That was a message that really hit home for all of us. So many of the farmers continue to struggle financially. The play helped remind us that we need to work together. Then and now."

"Are you talking about Value-X?"

Carrie shook her head. "Not only Value-X. We have more problems than just that. As you probably know, farm prices are low and have been for years. Most folks around here feel that no one appreciates the contribution of the small farmer anymore. A lot of people were demoralized by what was happening."

"Is it better now?"

"Yes, but only because farmers in the area have banded together. They still aren't getting decent prices for their crops, but they've found ways around that."

Carrie looked away; she had to swallow the lump in her throat. Her own family had been forced off the farm. The land had produced record yields, and it still wasn't enough to make ends meet. After several years of dismal wheat prices, the family had realized the farm could no longer support them all. That was when her parents and younger brothers had moved into town.

This had happened shortly after she'd filed for divorce. At first it had seemed inevitable that they'd have to sell the land, but then her two older brothers had decided to lease it. Pete and Tom were married by this time, and along with their wives, they'd made the decision to stay.

Buffalo Valley had started to show signs of new life — with the reopening of the hotel and bar, as well as Rachel's pizza restaurant. And Lindsay, of course, had brought fresh hope to the community in so many ways. . . .

Carrie's mother had come into a small inheritance, and her parents chose to invest it in a business. Buffalo Valley was badly in need of an all-purpose hardware store. Carrie's father felt confident that if people could shop locally, they would, so the family had risked everything with this venture. To date, it had been a wise choice, but now with the mega-chain threatening to swallow up smaller businesses, the Hendricksons were in grave danger of losing it all.

"The American farmer refuses to be discounted," Carrie said, clearing her throat. "When was the last time you purchased pasta?"

"Pasta? As in noodles?" Vaughn asked in a puzzled voice. "Not recently. What makes you ask?"

"Ever hear of Velma brand?"

"Can't say I have."

Carrie tucked her arm through his. "It's made with wheat grown right here in Buffalo Valley. Brandon Wyatt and Gage Sinclair are part of the program. A year ago they joined several other local farmers, including my brothers, and some not so local, and cut out the middleman."

"You mean a group of farmers decided to start their own pasta company?"

"That's exactly what I mean."

"Ingenious," Vaughn said. "Incredible. So that's what you were talking about when you said they'd found ways around the poor prices."

"Yeah. There's often a solution — but sometimes you have to find it yourself."

"Carrie."

Carrie looked up to see Lindsay and Gage Sinclair standing in the aisle near them.

Carrie started to make the introductions, then remembered that Vaughn had met Lindsay in the pharmacy two days before.

"Vaughn, this is my husband, Gage," Lindsay said.

Vaughn stood and held out his hand to Gage. He and Carrie made their way into the aisle.

146

"I understand you're an Airborne Ranger," Gage said.

"Was," Vaughn corrected.

The two men began a conversation about military life, and Lindsay stepped closer to Carrie.

"Thanks for getting us such great seats," Carrie said. Lindsay was a substitute teacher now but still worked on the play every year.

"No problem." Lindsay glanced pointedly at Vaughn. "How's it going?"

Carrie didn't know how to answer. Her divorce had devastated her, and since then she'd thrown herself into her studies, forging ahead, insulating her heart. She'd been protecting herself from any risk of pain, but at the same time she'd eliminated any hope of finding love. Then Vaughn entered her life. His patience with Hassie had touched her. His willingness to hear her concerns about the changes that seemed to be coming to Buffalo Valley inspired her to fight for what she knew was right.

Carrie looked at Vaughn and sighed. "He gives me hope," she whispered.

"I remember the first time I saw Gage," Lindsay whispered back. "He looked at me and . . . I know it's a cliché, but it was as if someone had zapped me with an electrical jolt. I didn't even know this man's name and it was as though I'd *connected* with him."

The music started and Gage reached for

Lindsay's hand. "We'd better find our seats."

Gage and Lindsay left, and Carrie and Vaughn returned to their own seats. No sooner had they settled in than the curtain went up.

Several times during the evening, Carrie caught Vaughn studying her. She felt his eyes on her, and when she turned to meet his gaze, he took her hand and entwined his fingers with hers. Carrie had the sensation that something was troubling him, but now wasn't the time to ask.

"Kids in high school actually wrote the play themselves?" Vaughn asked Carrie for the second time. He found it difficult to believe that a group of teenagers could have created and put on such a high-quality production. The acting was a bit amateurish, true, but the emotion and heart that went into each scene stirred him more than he would've thought possible.

After seeing the play, Vaughn realized he could no longer evade a decision regarding Value-X. Not after these vivid depictions of the struggles Buffalo Valley had faced. Through the years, bad weather and bouts of pestilence had plagued the land. The tales of the "dust bowl" years had given him a small taste of the hopelessness the farmers endured. The play ended with a farm family standing in the middle of a wheat field, their heads held high, their arms linked. Just thinking about that scene raised goose bumps on his arms.

"High-school kids," he repeated before Carrie could respond.

"It was as good as I said it was, don't you agree?"

Words fell short of describing the powerful sensation he'd experienced throughout the play.

"Would you like to come over to Buffalo Bob's for hot cider? A lot of folks do," Carrie said. "But I should warn you, Pete and Tom will be there."

Vaughn would enjoy going another round with Carrie's brothers, but unfortunately he had a long drive back to Grand Forks. "Another time," he told her. He wasn't in the mood to socialize.

As they stepped from the warmth of the theater into the cold night air, his breath became visible in foggy wisps. The cold seemed to press against him with an intensity he hadn't expected.

"Let me get you home," Vaughn said, placing his arm around her. He wasn't accustomed to cold so severe it made his lungs ache just to draw a breath.

Carrie wrapped her scarf more securely about her neck and pulled on her wool hat. Normally they would have walked the short distance, but not when the cold was so bitter, the wind so vicious.

Vaughn helped her into his rental car, then hurried around the front and climbed into the driver's seat.

Neither spoke as he drove the few short blocks to her family's home. Vaughn wondered if Carrie had realized no one would be there. The house was dark. Had he asked, she would've invited him inside, but he preferred talking to her there, in the dark.

"Carrie, listen, there's something I have to tell you." He stared straight ahead, unable to look at her.

"I know what you're going to say."

He jerked his gaze to hers. Her blue eyes were barely visible in the moonlight, but he saw enough to be aware that she only *thought* she knew.

"We've known each other a very short time," she said. "You'll be leaving soon."

"It doesn't have anything to do with you and me."

"Oh." He could hear her surprise and embarrassment. "I'm sorry. I didn't mean to speak out of turn."

"At the same time, it has *everything* to do with us," he said, and slid his arm around her neck and drew her to him. He breathed in her scent — clean and light and floral; he felt her body against him, softly yielding. After a moment of debating the wisdom of what he was about to do, he exhaled harshly.

"Vaughn, what is it?"

He didn't know where he'd find the courage to tell her. She raised her head to look at him, her eyes full of warmth and concern. Kissing her was wrong; he knew it even as he lowered his mouth to hers. He didn't care, he *had* to kiss her one last time before he was forced to watch the transformation that would come over her when she learned the truth. In a few seconds he was going to hurt and disillusion her.

His mouth was on hers with excitement, with need. The kiss was intense. Real. It seemed to him that the woman in his arms had flung open her life for him, and that thought left his senses reeling.

The guilt he felt was nearly overwhelming.

Her hat had fallen off, and Vaughn slipped his fingers into her hair. He held her close, refusing to release her. From the way she clung to him, she didn't want him to let her go.

"Tell me?" she pleaded.

"Carrie . . ." He shut his eyes and held his breath for a moment. "I came to Buffalo Valley for more reasons than you know."

"Hassie?"

"For Hassie, yes, but . . . I'd also been asked to check on something for a friend."

"Check on what?"

"The only way to say this is straight out. I work for Value-X."

Carrie froze. *"What?"* she asked, her voice confused. Uncomprehending.

"Value-X's corporate headquarters are in Seattle."

"I thought you were just discharged from the army."

"I was."

She pulled away from him and scraped the hair back from her face as though to see him more clearly. "I don't understand."

"I don't expect you to. I took a job with Value-X after my discharge."

"They sent you here?" Her back was stiff now, and she leaned away from him. A moment earlier she couldn't get close enough, and now she was as far from him as the confines of the vehicle would allow. "Are your parents involved in this?"

"No! They don't even know."

She shook her head over and over, raising both hands to her face. "I need to think," she said.

"I don't officially start with the company until January."

"You're a *spy?*"

"No. The vice president of new development asked me to check out the town. I was going to be in the area, anyway. It made perfect sense, and . . ."

"And so you did."

He couldn't very well deny it. "You have every right to be furious."

"You're damn straight I do," she said, grabbing the door handle.

Vaughn stopped her by reaching for her hand. "I can't do it."

She glared at him. "Can't do what?"

"Work for Value-X. I'm faxing in my resignation first thing tomorrow morning." No one would be in the office to read it until after Christmas, but that couldn't be helped.

Carrie still appeared stunned. "I don't know what to say," she muttered. "I need time to think."

"All right. I know this is a shock. I won't blame you if you decide you want nothing more to do with me. That decision is yours." He sincerely hoped his honesty would prove his sincerity.

She climbed out of the car and without another word, ran toward the house. Vaughn waited at the curb until she was safely inside and then, with a heavy heart, he drove back to Grand Forks.

His parents were still up, playing a game of Scrabble at the kitchen table, when he walked in.

His mother looked up and smiled. "How was the play?"

"Excellent," he answered.

His father picked up four new alphabet squares. "I heard it was put on by a bunch of kids."

"That's true, but they did an incredible

job." Vaughn turned a chair around and straddled it.

"How's Carrie?" his mother asked innocently enough.

Vaughn's response was so long in coming that Barbara frowned. She seemed about to repeat her question when he spoke, intending to forestall her.

"If no one minds," he said quickly, "I think I'll go to bed."

"Sure," his father said, concentrating on the game.

"You don't want a cup of tea first?" his mother asked, still frowning.

"I'm sure," he said.

Inside the guest room, Vaughn threw himself on the bed. The guilt and remorse that had haunted him on the sixty-minute drive from Buffalo Valley hadn't dissipated.

He folded his hands beneath his head and gazed up at the ceiling, his thoughts twisting and turning as he attempted to reason everything out. Now that Carrie knew the truth, he should feel better, but he didn't.

Resigning from Value-X was only a small part of what he had to do. He wouldn't be this attracted to Carrie if he truly loved Natalie. He closed his eyes and could only imagine what Natalie would say once she discovered what he'd done. Avoiding a confrontation with her would be impossible. She was coming to Buffalo Valley, and what was that old adage? *Hell hath no fury like a woman scorned.* He could feel the flames licking at his feet even now. Oh, yes, this was only the beginning.

He trusted that Carrie would eventually forgive him for his deception concerning Value-X and his role with the company. He'd been as candid with her as he could.

Unfortunately Value-X wasn't the only issue. He didn't have the courage to tell Carrie about Natalie. Not yet. He didn't want to force her to accept more than one disappointment at a time. Once she'd dealt with the fact that he was connected with Value-X, he'd explain his relationship to Natalie. By then, that relationship would be over.

Sitting up, Vaughn swung his legs over the side of the bed and sat there for several minutes. His mind wasn't going to let him sleep, so it was a waste of time to even try.

The kitchen light was off when he stepped into the hallway. He assumed his parents had finished their game and retired for the night. Perhaps if he had something to eat, it might help him relax. To his surprise, he found his father sitting in the darkened living room, watching the late-night news. The Christmas tree in the corner twinkled with festive lights that illuminated the gifts piled beneath.

"I thought you'd gone to bed," his father said.

"I thought I had, too," Vaughn answered, joining him. They both stared at the screen, although there was nothing on except a too-familiar commercial. Yet anyone might have thought they were viewing it for the first time.

His father suddenly roused himself and turned off the TV. "Something on your mind?" he asked after an uncomfortable moment of silence.

Vaughn hesitated, wondering if he should share his burden.

His father yawned loudly. "You'd better start talking soon if you're inclined to do so, because I'm about to hit the sack."

Vaughn laughed despite himself. "Go to bed. This is something I've got to settle myself."

"All right," Rick Kyle told him. "If you're sure . . ."

"Night, Dad," Vaughn said, grateful for having been raised by two loving parents.

"You coming to bed or not?" Gage Sinclair called to his wife. Lindsay had been fussing ever since they'd driven back to the farm. After they'd put the girls down for the night, she'd decided to sort laundry. Then it was something in the kitchen. He had no idea what she was up to now.

"Lindsay," he shouted a second time, already in bed himself.

"I'll be there in a minute." Her voice came from the living room.

"That's what you said fifteen minutes ago."

Tossing aside the comforter, he got out of bed and reached for his robe before walking into the other room. Sure enough, he found her sitting on the sofa, knitting. This particular project looked like it was going to be a sweater for Joy. "Tell me what's bothering you," he said, sinking down in his recliner.

"Things," she returned a moment later.

"You're not upset with me, are you?"

She lowered her knitting and stared at him. "Has there *ever* been a time I was afraid to tell you exactly what I thought, Gage Sinclair?"

Gage didn't have to consider that for very long. "No," he said decisively.

"Exactly."

"Then what is it?" he pressed. All at once he knew. The answer should have been obvious. "Value-X?"

His wife nodded. "My mind's been buzzing ever since I talked to the company. That woman was so arrogant. I don't doubt for a moment that Value-X will be as ruthless as they need to be."

"Sweetheart, there isn't anything we can do about it now."

"I know, but I can't stop thinking. We've got to get organized."

"I agree."

157

"It's just that with Christmas only a few days away, everyone's so busy we can't find even a couple of hours."

"That's what happens this time of year."

"But the future of the entire *town* is at risk."

"Don't you think other towns have tried to keep them out?" He didn't mean to be a pessimist, but truth was truth. No matter what kind of slant they put on it, nothing was going to change.

"What worries me most is Hassie's attitude," Lindsay admitted. "I've never known her to give up without one hell of a fight."

"Sweetheart, she's single-handedly slayed dragons for this town. It's someone else's turn."

"I know." This was said with a sadness that tugged at his heart. Gage knew his wife had a special relationship with Hassie. He also knew that without Hassie Knight, he might never have married Lindsay. Now it was impossible to imagine his life without her and their daughters. It wasn't anything he even wanted to contemplate.

"I saw you talking to Maddy," Gage said. The two women had been friends nearly all their lives, and they still relied on each other when either had a problem. This problem, though, was shared by the whole town. Predictably, Lindsay had taken on Buffalo Valley's latest dilemma — taken on Hassie's role, too, he thought.

That was what he loved about her, and at the same time dreaded. His wife didn't know the meaning of the word *no.* She simply refused to give up. When she'd first moved to Buffalo Valley, they'd been constantly at odds; he was crazy about her, yet couldn't say a word to her without an argument erupting.

They'd met one hot summer afternoon at Hassie's. Lindsay had left town but she'd stayed in his mind. For weeks afterward she filled his thoughts, and if that wasn't bad enough, she invaded his dreams. When he learned she'd accepted the teaching position at the high school, he managed to convince himself that this Southern belle wouldn't last longer than the first snowflake. His behavior toward her had been scornful, even combative — an attempt to keep from making a fool of himself. It hadn't worked, since he'd done a mighty fine job of looking like a dolt.

Then there was the matter of finding their aunt, the illegitimate child of her grandmother and his grandfather. Gage had wanted no part of that. He'd violently disagreed with her decision to intrude on this unknown woman's life.

He'd been wrong about that, and during the past few years, Angela Kirkpatrick had become an important figure in their lives.

It didn't stop there. Lindsay had known what was best for Kevin, too. His much younger brother was never meant to be a farmer. Kevin hated what Gage loved most. But Kevin's talent meant that he would one day be named among the country's major artists. Lindsay had recognized his brother's gift when Gage had turned a blind eye to it.

Having seen the error of his ways — repeatedly — Gage had come to trust his wife's judgment and intuition. "What do you suggest we do?" he asked, getting up and sitting next to her on the sofa.

"I just don't know, and neither does Maddy," Lindsay told him, shrugging helplessly. She put aside her knitting, muttering that she couldn't concentrate anymore. Not *his* fault, she assured him. It was just this Value-X thing.

He clasped her hand and she gripped his hard. She scrambled into his lap, pressing her head against his shoulder. Gathering her close, Gage savored the feel of his wife in his arms.

"I tried to talk to Hassie about it, but she said I should turn my thinking around and try to look at the positive side of the situation."

"Have you?" Gage asked, dropping a kiss on her forehead.

"No. I can't get past what'll happen to Buffalo Valley once Value-X arrives."

The prospects for the future weren't bright in view of what had become of other communities the retailer had entered.

Neither spoke for several moments, then Gage changed the subject. "I enjoyed meeting Vaughn Kyle."

"You two certainly seemed to hit it off."

"We got to talking about army life."

"Wouldn't it be wonderful if he moved to Buffalo Valley and he and Carrie got married?" his wife said. Sometimes he forgot what a romantic she could be. And yet . . . time and again, her instincts about people proved to be correct. She was the one who'd claimed Maddy and Jeb were falling in love, although Gage would've sworn on a stack of Bibles that it wasn't happening.

"Carrie and Vaughn?" he repeated.

"Mark my words, Gage."

Lindsay wasn't going to get an argument out of him. "You ready for bed now?"

"Ready," she told him, kissing his jaw and sending shivers down his back.

"Me, too," he whispered.

Chapter 8

"I've got a meeting in town this morning," Margaret Eilers announced at the breakfast table Saturday morning, three days before Christmas.

This came as news to Matt. His wife hadn't mentioned anything about going into Buffalo Valley. Something was in the air, though. The phone had been ringing off the hook for the better part of a week. He knew the women around here were up in arms about the Value-X problem, although Matt didn't see what could be done. Neither did any of the other men in town.

"Can you watch the kids for me, Sadie?" His wife smiled at the housekeeper, who'd been with the family since Margaret's childhood.

Sadie brought a stack of pancakes to the table and wiped her hands on her apron. "Not this morning," she said in that brusque way of hers.

Anyone who didn't know Sadie might assume she was put out by the request. She wasn't. This was simply her manner, and they were all used to it. Matt had learned

162

more than one lesson from the highly capable housekeeper. She'd become an ally and friend shortly after he married Margaret, and he was forever grateful for all she'd done to see him through his troubles.

"I'm leaving at noon, remember?" Sadie reminded them.

"That's right," Margaret muttered, glancing at Matt.

"What's going on in town?" he asked. Margaret wasn't one to make unnecessary trips, nor was she the type of woman to find an excuse to shop.

"I'm meeting with the other women. We're going to discuss ideas on how to deal with the threat from Value-X," she told him.

"Sweetheart, that's already been discussed to death. The town council has tried, Hassie's —"

"Everyone's been talking to Ambrose Kohn individually. We've got to mount a defense as a community."

"And do what? Sign petitions?" He didn't mean to sound negative, but he sincerely doubted that Value-X cared what the community thought. They'd already set the wheels in motion. Matt suspected many a town such as theirs had tried to mount a defense, but it had been hopeless from the start. Value-X knew how to win.

"We can't sit by and do nothing," Margaret insisted.

"But it's almost Christmas."

"Exactly, and Value-X is counting on the community to delay a response until after the holidays. By then it could be too late. That's what the meeting's about. I'm willing to fight now, and so are the other women in town."

"What about the men?"

"You're welcome to join us, but . . ."

"But the women are spearheading this."

"That's because none of you men believe it can be done." Her smile belied the sharpness of her words. "You can still come if you want."

"No, thanks," Matt said, waving a hand in dismissal. "I've got the kids to look after."

Margaret smiled and reached over to spear a hotcake with her fork. They'd been married three years, and Matt fell more in love with her every day. Times had been hard in the beginning, but it seemed that once they'd survived that rough period, they'd grown closer than ever. Of one thing Matt was certain — his wife brought out the very best in him. He loved her with an intensity that gave him strength.

"So I can leave Hailey and David with you?"

"I did have plans this morning, but they can wait." He'd hoped to finish the gift he was working on for Margaret. The antique rocker had belonged to her father. Matt had stumbled upon it in the loft up in the barn, and Sadie had told him its history. Joshua McKenna had repaired it earlier, and Matt had sanded and varnished the wood. Sadie had sewed new cushions for the seat and back. Matt had hoped to add a final coat of varnish that morning so it would be ready for Margaret on Christmas morning. Well . . . he'd have to find time tonight.

"I don't know what you women think you're going to accomplish," he said, "but if you sincerely believe it'll make a difference, then I'll do my part — and I'll wish you well."

Margaret thanked him with a brilliant smile, rose from the table and kissed him. The kiss was deep and full of promise. She was letting him know he'd be rewarded a hundred times over at a more appropriate hour.

Soon afterward Margaret headed into town. Once the kids were up, dressed and fed, Matt decided he wanted to know exactly what the women intended. Reaching for the phone, he called Jeb McKenna, his closest neighbor.

"Is Maddy gone, too?" he asked. Matt heard children crying in the background.

"I've got my hands full."

"Me, too," Matt confessed.

"Do you know what they're planning?" Jeb asked.

"I don't have a clue, but I'm sorry now

that I didn't go with her. They have great intentions, but what can they do that hasn't already been tried?"

"You signed the petition?"

"Along with everyone else in town," Matt told him.

"Buffalo Bob contacted the governor and asked for help."

"Did he hear back?" Now, that was promising.

"Not yet."

Matt sighed impatiently. "I feel like we should be there."

"I do, too."

"Daddy." Hailey tugged at his jeans. "Can we go to town and have a soda?"

Matt grinned at his daughter. "Just a minute, honey." What an inspiration. "I'll meet you at the soda fountain," Matt suggested. "That way we can keep the kids occupied and we can talk ourselves."

"Good idea," Jeb said.

Matt pushed a tape into the truck's console and sang Christmas songs with his children as he drove into town. When he parked outside Hassie's, he noticed several other vehicles there, too. The two youngsters followed him excitedly into the drugstore.

The soda fountain appeared to be the most popular place in town; Gage Sinclair was there with his two daughters, and Jeb McKenna had arrived ahead of him. So had

Brandon Wyatt and six-year-old Jason. Every stool at the fountain was occupied.

Matt acknowledged his friends with a quick nod.

"Hey, Matt," Jeb said in a jocular tone, "seeing that you called us together, I'm hoping you've come up with a few ideas to share."

"Me?" Matt glanced at Jeb, who shifted his weight. "I called a couple of the other guys, too. I think we made a mistake by taking such a negative attitude. Now the women are stuck trying to cope with the problem all by themselves."

The door opened and Dennis Urlacher walked in with his three-year-old son. Little Josh might be named after Sarah's father, but he was the spitting image of his own.

"I'm not late, am I?" Dennis asked, taken aback by the sight of all the children.

Leta was doing her best to keep up with orders, but she was obviously overwhelmed. As soon as she delivered one soda, she got an order for two more. Apparently Hassie was at the meeting over at Sarah's shop, as well. The men stood in a small circle while the children sat at the counter. Their joyous laughter made all the fathers smile, none more than Matt.

"So, does anyone have any ideas?" Dennis asked.

"Did you get anywhere with the governor's office?" Jeb asked Bob.

Bob shook his head. "I got the runaround. Reading between the lines, I could tell the politicians don't want to get involved in this fight. Buffalo Valley is on its own."

"Okay," Matt said, "maybe the politicians don't want to take sides in this issue, but there are plenty of other influential people who aren't afraid of challenging Value-X."

"Who?"

A flurry of names followed — writers and filmmakers and media personalities — along with a volunteer to contact each one immediately after the holidays. This was exactly the kind of pressure necessary to get the company's attention.

Soon the men were talking excitedly, their voices blending with those of their children. Various ideas were considered, discarded, put aside for research or further thought. The women were right — they had to become a united front.

"Do you seriously believe anyone at the corporate level will listen?" Gage asked. "They've dealt with organized opposition before."

Matt shrugged, although he suspected that if Margaret was the one doing the talking, those muck-a-mucks would soon learn she refused to be ignored. A smile formed on his face as he imagined Margaret standing before the conglomerate's board of directors. They'd listen, all right.

"What's so funny?" Brandon Wyatt asked.

"Nothing." Matt shook his head, dispelling the image.

"Joanie's been real upset about all this."

"Maddy, too," Jeb said. "I don't think the grocery will be too badly affected, but that's not the point. She's worried about how everyone else will fare."

"Value-X would ruin Joanie's and my business," Brandon said. "But I don't think a bunch of suits in some fancy office in Seattle really care what'll happen to a small video store in Buffalo Valley."

The other men agreed.

"We could hold a rally," Gage suggested.

"The women have already thought of that," Leta inserted, speaking from behind the counter. "They figured it wouldn't have enough impact unless we got major media coverage."

Several of the men nodded; others seemed prepared to argue.

"Hassie's probably got a few ideas," Gage said next. "When she comes back from the meeting, we'll —"

Leta broke in. "Hassie's not with the others," she informed them as she set a chocolate soda on the polished mahogany counter.

"She's not?" The question came from two or three men simultaneously, including Matt.

"Nope. She's at home this morning."

This was news to them all.

"Hassie's not with the other women?" Dennis repeated, frowning. "But . . ."

"How many of them are over at Sarah's, anyway?" Matt wanted to know.

"They're not at Sarah's," Dennis told them.

"Then where are they?" Matt had assumed that was where the women had met. Sarah had the most space for such a gathering.

"I think they're over at the church with Joyce Dawson," Brandon Wyatt said. "I'm not sure, but something Joanie said . . ."

Matt figured it wasn't all that important where the women had congregated. The community was coming together, bringing forth ideas. Value-X might be a powerful corporation, but the men and women of Buffalo Valley weren't going to submit humbly to this invasion.

Sleep had eluded Vaughn Kyle all night. The message of the Christmas play had stayed with him. A community standing together, enduring through hard times, its unique character created by that history of struggle and victory. Not *a* community, *this* community. Buffalo Valley.

His confession to Carrie after the performance had played no small part in his inability to sleep. Unfortunately Carrie wasn't the only woman he needed to talk to, and the conversation with Natalie would probably be even harder.

He waited until eight, Seattle time, before calling her. His decision to resign and the reasons for it would infuriate her. And his plan to end their relationship — he didn't even want to think about her reaction to that. He wasn't convinced that she truly loved him, but the humiliation of being rejected would be difficult for her to accept. He sighed; he'd betrayed Carrie twice over and now he was doing the same to Natalie.

The house was still quiet when Vaughn brought the portable phone into his room. Sitting on the bed, he dialed Natalie's home number and waited four long rings before she picked up.

"Hello." Her voice was groggy with sleep. Normally she'd be awake by now. He'd already started off on the wrong foot, and he had yet to say a word.

"I got you up, didn't I," he said.

"Vaughn," she said sleepily, then yawned. "Hello, darling."

Vaughn tried to ignore the guilt that rushed forward. Mere hours ago, he'd been holding and kissing Carrie.

"This is a surprise," Natalie cooed. "You must really be missing me."

"I need to talk to you about Value-X," Vaughn said, getting directly to the point. There was no easy way to do this.

"Now?" she protested. "You're always telling me all I think about is work. I didn't get home until after eleven last night, and work is the last thing I want to think about now. You know we're under a lot of pressure just before the holidays. There's so much I have to get done, especially since I'll be leaving on this trip."

"I do know, and I apologize." He honestly felt bad about this. "I'll be sending in a fax this morning."

She sighed as if to say she was already bored. "Why?"

He hesitated, bracing himself for her angry outburst. "I've resigned."

"*What?*" Her shriek was loud enough to actually startle him. "If this is a joke, Vaughn, I am *not* amused."

In some ways he wished it was. He doubted this was one of those situations he'd look back on years from now and find amusing. "You asked me to check out Buffalo Valley."

"So?" she asked. "You mentioned an aunt or someone you knew who lived there. What's the big deal?"

"The big deal is that the town isn't interested in Value-X setting up shop."

Natalie didn't so much as pause. "Honey, listen, we've already been through this. Few communities fully appreciate everything we can do for them. Invariably there's a handful

172

of discontented, ill-informed people who take it upon themselves to make a fuss. For the most part it's a token protest. Rarely is it ever a threat."

"If that's the case, why did you ask me to report back to you on Buffalo Valley?" She'd been worried, Vaughn knew; otherwise she'd never have suggested he check the place out.

"After the bad publicity in that Montana town, I overreacted. That was a mistake," she said quickly. "I see that now. A big mistake! I can't allow you to throw away the opportunity of a lifetime because I sent you into battle unprepared."

"Battle?"

"You know what I mean," she said irritably. "I wasn't thinking clearly. You were going to be in the area and it seemed like such a little thing. I should've known . . ."

"I'm grateful you asked me to do this," Vaughn countered. "I've learned a whole lot."

"No! No . . . this is all wrong." Natalie sounded desperate now.

"Buffalo Valley is a nice town. The people here are worried about what'll happen if Value-X moves in."

"But they don't understand that we —"

"They want someone to listen, and it's clear the company isn't going to do that." The purpose of Natalie's visit was to convince the people of Buffalo Valley that they needed Value-X.

"Of course the town wants us to listen, they all do, but what would happen to our jobs if we actually did?"

Natalie made her point without contradiction by Vaughn, although he doubted she recognized the real import of her words.

"Don't do anything stupid," Natalie pleaded. "At least wait until I get there and we can talk this out."

Her arrival was an entirely separate issue. "That brings up another . . . problem."

"Now what?" she snapped. "I suppose you're going to tell me you've met someone else and you want to dump me."

Vaughn rubbed his hand along his thigh and said nothing.

"This has *got* to be a joke." She gave a short, humorless laugh. "Talk about the Grinch stealing Christmas!"

"I realize my timing is bad —"

"Bad! You don't know the half of it."

"Natalie, listen, I'm genuinely sorry."

"You asked me to be your wife."

Technically, that wasn't true. They'd talked about marriage, but Natalie had shown no great enthusiasm. Now, however, didn't seem to be the time to argue the point. "If you'll recall, you were pretty lukewarm about the idea. That has to tell you something about your feelings for me."

"I was playing it cool," she insisted, sounding close to tears.

Vaughn had never known Natalie to cry, and he experienced deep pangs of regret. "I didn't mean to hurt you, but I had to say something before you showed up here." He hoped she'd cancel the trip, although he figured that was unlikely.

"I wanted you to be thrilled when I finally agreed to marry you. Now you're saying you don't love me."

"Not exactly . . ." He did hold tender feelings for her, but he knew with certainty that they were never meant to be together.

"You love me — but you love someone else more?"

Vaughn wasn't sure how to respond. He hadn't declared his feelings for Carrie, but the promise he felt with her outweighed his feelings for Natalie.

"I suppose she's one of the crusaders against Value-X. That would make sense, now that I think about it."

Vaughn didn't answer.

"I'm not giving up on us," Natalie insisted, "not until we've had a chance to speak face-to-face."

He'd already guessed she wouldn't make this easy. "I'd rather you just accepted my decision."

A painful pause followed. "Just what do you plan to do with your life if you resign from Value-X?" she demanded.

"I don't know." His future was as much a

mystery to him as it was to her. All Vaughn could say was that he had no intention of remaining with the company.

"You're not thinking clearly," Natalie said.

"Actually, I'm thinking about settling here." He wasn't sure where the words had come from, but until he said them aloud the possibility hadn't even occurred to him.

"In North Dakota," she blurted out, as though he was suffering from temporary insanity. "Now I *know* this is all a bad joke. Who in their right mind would live there? You know the demographics as well as I do. *No one* lives in a place like that on purpose."

"I would."

"This is ridiculous! I wouldn't believe it if I wasn't hearing it with my own ears. You can't be serious."

Although he knew it was probably a waste of breath, Vaughn felt obliged to tell her about Buffalo Valley. He wanted her to know the people he'd met. She couldn't begin to grasp what he felt unless she understood who and what they were.

"This farming community is small-town America at its best," he said, and wondered if she was even listening. "They have a history of banding together in hard times — and there've been plenty of hard times." He wanted to make her understand the depth of his respect for them, so he relayed to her the plot of the Christmas play.

"That's all very interesting," Natalie told him, her tone bored, "but that was then and this is now. Value-X will come into Buffalo Valley with or without you. With or without me. It doesn't matter how many times you sit and watch a group of teenagers act out the town's history, nothing is going to change."

"It will," Vaughn said.

"I'm not letting you quit. One day you'll thank me."

"Natalie, what are you doing?"

"First I'm going into corporate headquarters to make sure no one reads your resignation letter. Then I'm flying out on the twenty-seventh, just the way I planned, so we can talk this out."

"I wish you wouldn't. Let it go, Natalie."

Her returning laugh sounded like a threat. "I don't think so. You didn't really believe I'd allow you to cut me loose with a simple phone call, did you?"

He didn't bother to respond. What was the point?

"You see yourself as this hero, this knight in shining armor, and while that's fine and good, it isn't going to work."

Vaughn could see the storm clouds gathering on the horizon.

Sunday morning while his parents attended church, Vaughn drove into Buffalo Valley. He'd made the trek so often in the past week that it seemed almost second nature to head in that direction.

Everything about the town appealed to him. It'd started when he'd first met Hassie and accepted the gold watch that had belonged to her husband. With the watch came an implied trust. He refused to be part of anything that would betray their relationship.

He hadn't heard from Carrie, but he would once she was ready. He didn't think it would take her long to come to terms with his confession. Because of her ex-husband's betrayal, it was vital that he be as open and honest with her as possible. However . . . he still hadn't explained Natalie's role in his life. Poor Carrie was about to be hit with a second shock, but there wasn't a damn thing he could do to prevent it.

He parked just outside town, at the twenty-acre site for the proposed Value-X. With the wind howling, he climbed out of the car and walked onto the property. Either he was becoming accustomed to the bone-chilling weather or it'd warmed up in the past twenty-four hours. He discovered he could breathe now without feeling as though he was inhaling ice particles.

He'd been there for several minutes when he saw a truck pull up and park next to his vehicle. Two men climbed out and started toward him. He instantly recognized them as Carrie's younger brothers.

"Chuck and Ken, right?" he said as they approached.

Chuck, the older of the two, touched his hat. "Vaughn Kyle?"

Vaughn nodded.

"Did you have a falling-out with Carrie after the play?" Chuck asked. The man was nothing if not direct. His brow had furrowed and the teasing friendliness was gone. "You hurt her and you have me to answer to."

"I have no intention of hurting her."

"Good." He nodded once as if to suggest the subject was closed.

"What are you doing out here?" Ken muttered.

Vaughn wasn't sure what to tell him. He hadn't asked Carrie to keep the fact that he was employed by Value-X a secret, but it was apparent that she had. If either Chuck or Ken knew the truth, they'd have him tarred and feathered and run out of town.

"Just looking," Vaughn told him.

"Looking at what? Empty land?"

"If you had this twenty acres or any portion of it, how would you develop it?" Vaughn asked the pair.

"That's easy," Ken said. "This town needs a feed store — been needing one for years. Most everyone has to drive to Devils Lake for their feed."

A feed store. Now that was interesting. "Why don't you do it?" he suggested.

179

"No time. The hardware store keeps us busy. Dad needs us there, but if someone were to come along with enough investment capital and a head for business, they'd be guaranteed success."

"Dad carries some of the more common feed, but he doesn't have room for much."

"We got to talking about a feed store just the other day," Ken said, glancing at his brother. "Wondering who might be able to open one."

This morning, Vaughn had casually told Natalie that he might settle in Buffalo Valley. A few days earlier his future was set, and now all at once he was cast adrift. His carefully ordered life was in shambles, and Vaughn didn't like the uncomfortable feeling that gave him.

"It'd take someone with ready cash," Ken told him, his expression pensive, "and that's in short supply around here." He kicked at the snow with the toe of his boot. "People in these parts invest everything in their land."

"You interested?" Chuck asked him bluntly.

Vaughn looked in the direction of town, suddenly aware that this venture piqued his interest. He wanted to be part of Buffalo Valley, part of its future. It'd be a risk, but he'd never backed down from a challenge before and he wasn't planning to start now.

"I don't know a damn thing about running

a feed store," he said, meeting the other men's eyes.

Chuck and Ken studied him for a long moment.

"You serious about this?" Chuck finally asked.

Vaughn nodded.

"Between Dad, me and my brothers, we could show you everything you need to know."

"You'd do that?" Vaughn found it hard to believe that these men, who were little more than strangers, would willingly offer him their expertise.

"I saw a light in my sister's eyes that hasn't been there since her divorce," Ken told him. "That made me decide you might be worth taking a chance on." He stared down at the ground, then raised his head. "Now, I realize you moving into town and opening a feed store might have absolutely nothing to do with Carrie. Personally, I hope it does, but I want you to know that whatever happens between you and my sister is your business."

"That's the way it would have to be."

Her two brothers shared a glance and seemed to reach the same conclusion. "You're right about that." Chuck spoke for the pair. "This has nothing to do with Carrie."

"There are a lot of *ifs* in all this," Vaughn reminded them. He could see that they were getting excited, but then so was he. Naturally, all of this depended on a dozen different factors. Right now it was little more than the glimmer of an idea. Little more than a possibility. But it gave him a glimpse of what he might do. . . .

"At the moment the future doesn't look all that promising for Buffalo Valley," Ken said, surveying the bare land around them. It went without saying that if Value-X came to town, that would be the end of any talk about a feed store.

On the verge of leaving, Vaughn returned to the subject of their sister. "Have either of you seen Carrie?"

"She's gone for the day," Ken told him.

"All day?"

Chuck shrugged. "She's over with our brother Tom and his family. Did you two have plans?"

"No." How could he expect her to be at his beck and call? "I'll talk to her later," he said with reluctance. Their conversation had to take place soon. He'd rather this business with Natalie was over, but it now seemed that would require a protracted . . . discussion, for lack of a better word.

"She was upset when you dropped her off at the house after the play." Ken frowned at him in an accusatory way, suggesting Vaughn had some explaining to do. "What happened? What did you do?"

"That's Carrie's and my business. Remember?"

Chuck agreed. "She'd have our heads if she knew we were talking to you about her. We'll stay out of it, but like I said, you hurt her and you'll have me to answer to."

Vaughn nodded and resisted the urge to laugh. Melodramatic though they sounded, her brothers were serious.

"I heard you and your parents are spending Christmas Day with Hassie," Ken said.

News sure traveled fast in a small town. "We're coming for dinner."

"Then I think we might be able to arrange something." The two brothers exchanged another look.

"Arrange what?" Vaughn asked.

"Nothing much, just an opportunity for you to have some time alone with our sister." Chuck and Ken left then, both of them grinning broadly.

Chapter 9

Hassie spent Christmas morning with Buffalo Bob, Merrily and little Bobby, upstairs at the 3 of a Kind. Sitting around the Christmas tree with the family reminded her of what it'd been like years ago, when Valerie and Vaughn were young. The good feelings started right then, and she suspected this would be her best Christmas in a very long while.

Bobby's eyes got round as quarters when his father rolled out a shiny new miniature bicycle with training wheels. It amazed her that a three-year-old could actually ride a bicycle. In another three or four months, the park would be crowded with kids on bikes, enjoying the Dakota sunshine. When Hassie closed her eyes, she could almost hear the sound of their laughter. That would happen, she comforted herself, with or without Value-X.

She exchanged gifts with the family — magazine subscriptions for Bob and Merrily, a book of nursery rhymes for Bobby. Their gift to her was a new pair of lined leather gloves. After coffee and croissants — and hugs and kisses — she left.

Home again, Hassie set the dining-room table with her finest china. Not much reason to use it these days. Yet twice this week she'd had cause to bring it out of the old mahogany cabinet. The first time was her visit with Barbara and now Christmas dinner.

Already the kitchen counter was crowded with a variety of food. Carrie and her mother had thoughtfully dropped off a platter of decorated sugar cookies. Those cookies, plus the ones she'd collected the night of the exchange, added up to enough for the entire town.

Sarah Urlacher and Calla had given her a plate of homemade fudge. Maddy, Lindsay and several of the other women had stopped by with offerings, too — preserves and homemade bread and mincemeat tarts. It was far more than Hassie could eat in two or three Christmases.

Then word had leaked out about Vaughn Kyle and his parents coming for dinner. Before Hassie could stop them, her friends and neighbors had dropped off a plethora of side dishes. Joanie Wyatt sent over baked yams. Rachel Quantrill delivered a green-bean-and-cauliflower casserole. Soon all that was required of Hassie was the bird and dressing. The tantalizing aroma of baking turkey, sage and onions drifted through the house.

Living alone, Hassie didn't bother much

with meals. At night, after she closed the pharmacy, her dinner consisted of whatever was quick and easy. When Jerry had been alive and the children still lived at home, she'd been an accomplished cook. Now she considered cooking for one a nuisance. Many a night she dined on soup or a microwave entrée.

The doorbell chimed at exactly one o'clock, and Hassie, who'd been occupying herself with last-minute touches, was ready to receive her company.

"Merry Christmas," Barbara Kyle sang out, hugging Hassie as soon as she opened the front door.

"Merry Christmas. Merry Christmas." Hassie hugged them all.

For the next few minutes the men made trips back and forth between the car and the house. They hauled in festively wrapped presents, plus various contributions to the meal, including three beautiful pies.

"How in heaven's name are the four of us going to eat all these pies?" Hassie asked, giggling like a schoolgirl over such an embarrassment of riches. Pies, cookies, candies. Oh, my, she'd be on a diet till next June if she tasted everything in her kitchen.

"Pecan pie is Rick's favorite," Barbara explained.

"Pumpkin is mine," Vaughn said.

"And fresh apple mixed with cranberry is

mine," Barbara said, setting down the third pie. She had to rearrange other dishes on the crowded counter to find room for it.

"Apple mixed with cranberry," Hassie mused aloud. "That sounds delicious."

"I'm willing to share," Barbara said with a laugh.

The meal was even better than Hassie had dared hope. The turkey was moist and succulent, and the sage dressing was her finest ever, if she did say so herself. The four of them sat around the table and passed the serving dishes to one another. They talked and laughed as if each was part of Hassie's family. Anyone seeing them would never have guessed there'd been a thirty-three-year lapse in their relationship.

This was the way Christmas was meant to be, Hassie thought, immersing herself in the good feelings. Barbara had always been a talker, and she effortlessly kept the conversation going. The years had changed Rick Kyle considerably, Hassie noted, smiling over at him. She doubted she would've recognized him now.

The last time Hassie had seen Rick, he'd had shoulder-length brown hair, a bushy mustache and narrow-rimmed glasses. A wooden peace sign had dangled from his neck. As she recalled, he'd worn the craziest color combinations with tie-dyed bell-bottom jeans and sandals.

His hair was mostly gone now, but Barbara claimed bald men could be exceedingly sexy. Hassie wouldn't know about that, but it did her good to see that they were happy and obviously still in love.

Perhaps it was selfish of her, but she liked to believe that if her son had lived, Vaughn would've found the same happiness with Barbara.

"If I eat another bite, I swear someone might mistake me for a stuffed sausage," Barbara declared, pushing back her chair.

"Me, too." Rick wrapped his arms around his belly and groaned.

Hassie looked at Vaughn, who winked and said, "Could someone pass me the mashed potatoes and gravy?"

Laughing, Barbara hurled a roll at him from across the table. Vaughn deftly caught it. "Hey, I'm a growing boy."

When they'd finished, the men cleared off the table and Hassie brewed a pot of coffee. They gathered in the living room around the small Christmas tree, where Hassie had tucked three small gifts, one for each of her guests. Shopping in Buffalo Valley was limited and there hadn't been much time, so Hassie had found items with special meaning to share with her friends. Three little gifts she knew each would treasure.

For Barbara, it was a pearl pin Jerry had given her after Vaughn's birth. For Rick it was a fountain pen — an antique. Choosing a gift for Vaughn had been difficult. In the end she'd parted with one of the medals the army had awarded her son for bravery. Since Vaughn had recently been in the military himself, she felt he'd appreciate what this medal represented.

They seemed truly touched by her gifts. Barbara's eyes brimmed with tears and she pinned the pearl to her silk blouse. Rick, who didn't appear to be the demonstrative sort, hugged her. And Vaughn seemed at a loss for words.

"I have something to tell you," Vaughn said after several minutes of silence.

"This sounds serious." Hassie saw the look Barbara and Rick exchanged and wondered at its meaning.

Vaughn leaned forward and took Hassie's hands in both his own. "I told Mom and Dad earlier, and they urged me to be honest with you, as well. First, I want you to know I'd never deliberately do anything to hurt you."

"I know that. Honest about what?"

"Value-X. When I left Seattle, I'd accepted a job with them."

Hassie gasped, and her hand flew to her mouth. This was almost more than she could take in. Vaughn an employee of Value-X?

"I knew the company was planning to expand into Buffalo Valley, but I didn't understand the threat they represented to the community."

"He isn't working for them any longer," Barbara quickly inserted.

"Since I wasn't going to be officially an employee until after the first of the year, one of the vice presidents suggested I not mention my association with the company," Vaughn explained. "It was never my intention to deceive you or anyone in Buffalo Valley." He took a deep breath. "I faxed in my resignation and made it effective immediately."

Hassie felt a little dizzy. It was hard enough to grasp what he was saying, and she could only imagine what Carrie must think, so she asked, "Does Carrie know?"

Vaughn nodded. "I told her the night of the play. I didn't want to wait until after the holidays."

"What did she say?" Hassie asked. She feared that the news might mean the end for this budding relationship, which would be a dreadful shame.

"I haven't had a chance to speak to her since."

Barbara moved forward to the edge of the sofa. "There's more."

Vaughn cast his mother a look that suggested he'd rather she hadn't said anything.

"Tell me." As far as Hassie was concerned, it was too late for secrets now.

Vaughn glanced at his mother again. "I

don't want to get anyone's hopes up, because it's much too soon."

"Yes, yes, we know that," Barbara interjected, then waited for him to continue.

Vaughn's reluctance was evident. At last he said, "I'm investigating the possibility of opening a feed store here in town."

For the second time in as many moments, Hassie gasped. Only this time, the shock was one of excitement and pleasure. "Oh, Vaughn, that's an excellent idea. The town could use a feed store."

Rick wrapped his arm around his wife's shoulders, and both of them smiled broadly. "Vaughn spoke with two of the Hendrickson brothers about it yesterday morning," Barbara said. "They actually suggested it."

Hassie's heart surged with hope. Vaughn was right of course; there was no reason to get carried away. But she couldn't help it. The thought of having Vaughn right here in Buffalo Valley — she was almost afraid to believe it could happen.

"I've got an appointment with Heath Quantrill first thing Wednesday morning," Vaughn explained. "I'll need to put together a business plan and look into financing. The Hendricksons recommended I start there."

"Yes — Heath will give you good advice." Some of the excitement left her as reality came rushing back. "Everything hinges on what happens with Value-X, doesn't it?"

"True." Vaughn gave her a lopsided smile. "But I have a good feeling about this." As Hassie fought the emotion that threatened to overwhelm her, he added, "I want to invest in Buffalo Valley."

Keeping the tears at bay was impossible now. "Why would you do such a thing?" she asked between sniffles. Reaching into her pocket, she withdrew a linen handkerchief and blew her nose. She must be getting old, because normally she wasn't a woman prone to tears.

"I arrived in North Dakota thinking I knew exactly what I wanted and where I was headed," Vaughn said, "but everything changed. I probably shouldn't have said anything about my idea." He frowned at his mother. "But now that it's out, I'm glad you know."

"God bless you," Hassie whispered, stretching her arms toward Vaughn for a hug. Their embrace was warm. "If God had seen fit to give me a grandson, I would have wanted him to be just like you."

"That's a high compliment," Vaughn said, sitting down again.

"I meant it to be," Hassie told him. She rubbed her wet cheek with the back of her hand. "Look what you did," she said. "It isn't just anyone who can make this old lady weep."

"Shame on you, son," Rick teased, and they all smiled.

It took Hassie a few moments to compose herself.

"Look," Barbara said, pointing outside, "it's snowing."

Sure enough, the flakes were falling thick and soft, creating a perfect Christmas scene. "This is the way I always dreamed Christmas would be," Hassie whispered. "Surrounded by family —" she used the word purposely "— on a beautiful winter day."

This was the best Christmas she'd had in many years, and all because of the Kyles — people who'd been brought into Hassie's life by her son. Somehow she could picture Vaughn smiling down, wishing them a Merry Christmas.

Hassie had invited Carrie to join Vaughn and his parents for dessert on Christmas Day, and Carrie had yet to decide if she'd go. Vaughn's confession about working for Value-X had shocked her. The fact that he'd come into town, gained her confidence and that of everyone else — so he could collect information for the company — had been a betrayal of trust and goodwill. He'd withheld the truth from her and she should be outraged. She *was* outraged.

All week Vaughn had listened to everyone's objections to Value-X and said nothing. As she thought back on their numerous conversations, she realized how often he'd defended the company. At the time she'd assumed he was playing devil's advocate. Now she knew otherwise. Carrie wasn't sure what had happened to make him resign. Whatever it was, she was grateful. Still . . .

Trust was a basic issue with Carrie. Vaughn had betrayed her, Hassie and the entire town, and she couldn't conveniently look the other way. *Forgive and forget* might work for others, but not for her.

She didn't think Vaughn had told anyone else. Carrie hadn't determined whether that was a good thing or not. She did know she had to hide this from Hassie, who would be heartbroken if she found out. If she didn't show up at Hassie's and then claimed she'd forgotten, Hassie would immediately conclude that something was wrong. Then she'd start asking questions. Questions Carrie didn't want to answer. She could invent plausible excuses, but the problem was that Carrie *did* want to see Vaughn again, despite what he'd told her.

She needed to talk to him, needed to vent her feelings. The shock of his confession had robbed her of that chance. But finding a private time to speak with him today might prove difficult, if not impossible. In any event, she hadn't given verbal shape to her emotions yet. Talking to him should probably wait, she rationalized.

"Where you going?" Ken asked, following

her into the hallway as she gathered her coat, gloves and scarf.

"I bet she's going off to see that new friend of hers," Chuck teased.

"I'm going over to Hassie's," she informed her two younger brothers smugly.

"I suppose *he's* there."

How Pete knew that, Carrie could only guess. She shoved her arms into the silk-lined sleeves of her coat.

"He's there, all right," Tom said, leaning against the door jamb. "His car's parked outside Hassie's."

Carrie ignored him and went to get her purse. She and Hassie had exchanged their gifts on Christmas Eve, but Carrie had borrowed a book on traditional remedies that she needed to return. She retrieved it from the bookcase.

"Will you guys leave me alone?" she cried. All four of her brothers were trailing her from room to room. "Don't you have anything better to do?"

Her brothers glanced at each other and shrugged, then Pete announced, "Not really."

"Do you want to hear what we think of your new boyfriend?" Ken asked.

If they could be this obstinate, so could she. "No."

Carrie headed for the front door. If her four guardian angels wanted to follow her into the cold and snow, that was their choice.

"I like him, Carrie," Ken called after her.

"Me, too." Tom crowded beside him in the doorway.

"He's all right," Pete concurred.

Chuck simply winked and gave her a thumbs-up. This had to be a record. Never before had she dated a man all four of her brothers approved of. Little did they know. She wondered what they'd say if they knew that, until recently, he'd been a Value-X employee. The answer didn't bear considering. She couldn't disillusion them any more than she could Hassie. Against her will, she'd been pulled into his subterfuge, and she hated it.

The snow was falling hard by the time Carrie reached Hassie's house; she barely noticed.

Vaughn answered the door and surprised her by closing it after him as he stepped onto the porch. "Merry Christmas," he said, his eyes never leaving hers.

As much as possible, she avoided looking at him.

"We need to talk, Carrie."

"Here? Now?" She faked a short laugh. "I don't think so, Vaughn."

"Later, then?"

She nodded.

He sighed with unmistakable relief. "Thank you."

She didn't *want* to feel anything. She longed to ignore him, make a token visit and

196

then be on her way. But it was too late for that. Her emotions were painfully confused; she wanted to kiss him and at the same time, she wanted to scream and rage and throw his betrayal in his face.

He pressed his hand to her cheek. "I'm glad you're here."

She'd intended to slap his hand away, but instead, her fingers curled around his, and she closed her eyes and leaned toward him. Then she was angry with herself for being weak and jerked back.

"Come in out of the cold," Hassie called just as Vaughn opened the door and Carrie stepped inside. She took off her coat and tossed it onto the stair railing.

"Have you met my dad?" Vaughn asked, taking Carrie by the elbow and escorting her into the living room. He made the introductions.

"Pleased to meet you," she said, hoping none of the stiffness she felt came through in her voice.

Hassie was on her way to the kitchen. "You're just in time for pie."

"I'll help dish up," Barbara said, following Hassie.

"Me, too," Carrie offered, eager to escape Vaughn.

Barbara Kyle shook her head. "We'll take care of it."

The two older women disappeared, which

meant that Carrie was left alone with Vaughn and his father. She would've preferred the women's company and felt awkward alone with the two men. Vaughn was obviously eager to talk to her, and she was just as eager to avoid any conversation with him. Yes, there were things she needed to say; she wasn't ready, though — not nearly ready. She glanced in his direction and he mouthed something, but she looked away.

"Hassie and Barb are trying to keep you and Vaughn together," Rick confided to her frankly. Vaughn scowled fiercely. "So you may as well play along," he advised. "Here, sit down, Carrie, and make yourself comfortable."

She sat on the sofa and Vaughn joined her, sitting so close that their thighs brushed. In an effort to ignore him, she stared out the picture window.

"Isn't it a lovely day?" she asked, making conversation with his father. "The snow —" A flash of color outside caught her attention. It was her younger brothers. Gasping, she leaped to her feet.

"What?" Vaughn asked, getting up, too.

"It's Chuck and Ken," she said, and pointed at the window. Sure enough, they were outside — in an old-fashioned sleigh pulled by two draft horses.

"That's my great-great-grandfather's sleigh," Carrie explained. "He used it to deliver the mail. Dad and Mr. McKenna have been fixing it up. It's been in the barn for the last hundred years."

"That sleigh looks like something straight out of a Christmas movie," Vaughn's father remarked, standing by the window. "Whose horses are they?"

"I think they belong to a friend of Pete's," Carrie said.

Despite her mood, she giggled. Her brothers must have planned this all along. How they'd managed to keep it a secret she could only guess.

The doorbell chimed, and when Hassie answered it, she found Chuck grinning down at her.

"Anyone here interested in a sleigh ride?" he asked, looking around Hassie to where Carrie and Vaughn stood. "There's room for five."

"I'm game," Rick said. "Come on, Barb."

"Hassie?" Vaughn turned to their hostess.

She seemed about to refuse, then smiled broadly and said, "Don't mind if I do."

Vaughn helped Hassie on with her coat and made sure her boots were tightly laced before they ventured outside. Carrie tried not to be affected by the tenderness he displayed toward Hassie, especially when he bent down on one knee to lace her boots. There was nothing condescending in his action, only affection and concern. Meanwhile, Rick held

Carrie's coat for her and then Barbara's. By the time they left the house, the old sleigh, pulled by twin chestnut geldings, had attracted quite a bit of attention from the neighborhood. The horses were festively decked out in harnesses decorated with jangling bells.

Barbara, Rick and Hassie sat in the back seat, which fortunately was nicely padded. Once they were settled, Ken handed them a blanket to place over their laps. Carrie and Vaughn took the front seat, which was narrower and made of wood, forcing them close together.

Chuck and Ken walked in front of the horses, leading them down the unfamiliar street.

"Where are you taking us?" Carrie shouted as her brothers climbed onto the sleigh.

"The park," Ken called back.

"Shouldn't we be singing Christmas songs?" Barbara asked.

"Go right ahead," Rick answered, and taking him at his word, Vaughn's mother started with "Jingle Bells." What could be more fitting? Even if it was a "two-horse open sleigh."

Moments later Hassie's rough voice joined Barbara's soft soprano.

Carrie began to sing, too, and soon Vaughn's rich baritone blended with the women's voices. He and Carrie looked at each other. Perhaps it was the magic of the season or the fact that they were in a sleigh singing while they dashed through the snow, their song accompanied by the muffled clopping of hooves and the jingling of harness bells. Whatever the reason, Carrie realized her anger had completely dissipated. Vaughn seemed to genuinely regret what he'd done. He wasn't involved in a plot to destroy Buffalo Valley. To his credit, as soon as he'd recognized the threat Value-X represented to the town, he'd resigned from the company. It couldn't have been easy to walk away from a high-paying job like that.

Vaughn noticed the transformation in her immediately. He stopped singing and leaned close enough to ask, "Am I forgiven?"

Carrie nodded.

His eyes brightened and he slid an arm around her shoulders. Carrie was convinced that if their circumstances had been different, he would've kissed her.

When they reached the middle of the park, they found Carrie's entire family waiting there, applauding their arrival.

Effortlessly they segued from one Christmas carol to another. Everyone seemed to have a favorite. Amid the singing and the laughter, Carrie's mother served hot chocolate from large thermoses.

Vaughn and Carrie left their places in order to give others an opportunity to try out the sleigh. After several trips around the park, Chuck and Ken drove Hassie and Vaughn's parents back to Hassie's. Carrie and Vaughn remained with her family.

With pride, Carrie took Vaughn around and introduced him to everyone he had yet to meet.

"What were Chuck and Ken talking about earlier?" Tom asked, standing next to his wife, Becky.

Vaughn glanced at Carrie. "We discussed a few ideas, nothing more."

"That's not what I understood," Tom said. "Chuck said you'd made an appointment to talk to Heath Quantrill."

"You've got an appointment to see Heath?" Carrie asked. "About what?" She'd suspected earlier that something was up involving her two younger brothers. Sunday night they'd sat with their father at the kitchen table, talking excitedly in low voices. Carrie couldn't figure out what they were doing, and when she asked, their replies had been vague.

Rather than answer her directly, Vaughn looked away.

"More secrets?" she asked him under her breath.

"Vaughn's thinking about opening up a feed store in town," Tom supplied.

"Is this true?" she asked. If so, it was the best kind of secret.

"Nothing's certain yet," he told her, and she could see that he wasn't pleased with her older brother for sharing the news. "Everything's just in the planning stages. The *early* planning stages."

"You'd actually consider moving to Buffalo Valley?"

Vaughn nodded and smiled down on her, but then his gaze clouded. "I still need to talk to you."

"Of course."

"Privately," he insisted.

The park was crowded with her family. Carrie knew that the instant they broke away, one of her brothers or nieces and nephews would seek her out. "We can try," she promised.

"It's important."

Her heart was in her eyes, but Carrie didn't care if he saw that or not. "I'm so excited you might move here."

"I'm excited, too."

He didn't sound it. If anything, he seemed anxious. "What is it?" she asked. She wanted to hear what he needed to say, and she wanted to hear it *now*, even if they couldn't escape her family.

"Someone from Value-X is coming to Buffalo Valley," he murmured.

"You mean the representative Lindsay mentioned?" Carrie was well aware that the company intended to wage a public-relations campaign to win over the community; that was part of their strategy. She suspected the corporate heads at Value-X had only the slightest idea how unwelcome the retailer was in Buffalo Valley. Whatever they were planning simply wouldn't work.

"Yes. Her name's Natalie Nichols and —"

"It doesn't matter," she told him.

"Yes, it does," he countered.

Carrie lowered her voice, wanting him to know he could trust her. "I didn't tell anyone — no one knows."

"Hassie does. I told her myself."

She didn't understand what had prompted that confession, but wasn't sure it had been the wisest thing.

"She deserves honesty, the same way you do." Vaughn's brow creased with concern. "I would've come to meet her, with or without Value-X."

"I know."

"It isn't going to be pretty, Carrie, when Natalie Nichols arrives. Value-X has proved that it's capable of bulldozing its way into a town. They've done it before."

"Not here, not in Buffalo Valley. We won't let it happen." When he shook his head, she whispered, "It's going to be all right, Vaughn." Because her fears about him had been laid to rest, she leaned forward and kissed him.

Vaughn wrapped his arms around her and held her close.

"Hey, what's this?" Pete shouted.

Carrie laughed. "Leave us be," she replied. "Go on! Shoo!" She wasn't about to let her brothers ruin the most romantic moment of her life.

"Never," Tom hollered.

"There's something else," Vaughn said, ignoring her brothers.

"I have a feeling it's going to have to wait," she said, and ducked just in time to miss a flying snowball. Vaughn, however, wasn't quick enough. Snow exploded across his shoulder and he whirled around to face four large Hendrickson males.

"You shouldn't have done that," he said mildly.

"You gonna make me sorry?"

"Oh, yeah." Vaughn's chuckle was full of threat. "Prepare to die, Hendrickson."

Three hours later a cold and exhausted Vaughn made his way back to Hassie's. The snowball fight had eventually involved everyone in Carrie's large family, from two-year-old Eli to his grandfather. They'd stopped only long enough to build snow forts before the battle had resumed with peals of laughter and more hilarity than Vaughn could remember in years.

He'd sincerely meant to tell Carrie about his relationship with Natalie, but the opportunity never arose again. It became easy to let it ride once they were caught up in the family fun. Come morning, he was driving back to town to meet with Heath; he'd stop by the pharmacy and tell her then.

It was dark when he returned to Hassie's, and his parents were ready to head home to Grand Forks. When they got there, he discovered that Natalie had left five messages on his parents' machine. He was stunned to learn that she'd already arrived in North Dakota.

The first message, from the Seattle airport, had been soft and coaxing, claiming she needed to speak to him at his earliest convenience. By the final one, her tone had become hard and demanding. The last part of the message, telling him she'd call early the next morning, had sounded more than a little annoyed.

"Trouble?" his father asked, standing next to the phone as the message finished playing.

Vaughn shook his head. "Nothing I can't handle."

"Good."

"This has been the most wonderful Christmas," his mother said as she turned off the lights. They all went to bed, wishing each other good-night and a final Merry Christmas.

The following morning Vaughn woke early. He showered, shaved and dressed for his meeting with Heath. Sooner or later, he'd have to talk to Natalie, but he wanted as much information as he could gather before the inevitable confrontation. He gulped down a cup of coffee, eager to be on his way, to begin this new phase of his life. His mother hugged him before he left. "What do you want me to say if Natalie shows up?"

"No need to tell her anything," he advised. He'd deal with her when he had to, but not before. The letter she'd mentioned would be in the community post office soon and with that, the campaign would officially start. Vaughn was prepared to do whatever was necessary to keep the retailer out of Buffalo Valley. He had a stake in the town's future now.

He parked near the bank, then hurried inside; to his surprise, Heath's glass-enclosed office looked empty. "I have an appointment with Mr. Quantrill," Vaughn told the receptionist.

"You're Mr. Kyle?"

Vaughn nodded.

"Mr. Quantrill left a message. He had some last-minute business to attend to and said I should reschedule the appointment. He sent his apologies and asked me to tell you that the Kohn property has sold."

It wasn't until he was standing outside that Vaughn understood the significance of the message. The Kohn property was the land Value-X wanted. So the battle lines had been drawn. No wonder Quantrill was out of the office. There was no longer any reason for Vaughn to meet with him; Quantrill and the community had far more important issues to worry about.

Vaughn walked over to the pharmacy, his steps slow. No doubt Hassie and everyone else in town had heard the news. He knew how discouraged they'd be.

When he entered the pharmacy, Carrie was behind the prescription counter. As the bells over the door cheerfully announced his arrival, she glanced up, and from her disheartened expression, it was clear she'd heard. Her eyes seemed dull and lifeless. For a long moment she stared at him, almost as though he was a stranger.

"I guess you know?" he asked, stepping toward her.

"Oh, yes," she said with such sadness it nearly broke his heart.

"I'll help, Carrie," he told her. "We can beat Value-X if we stand together." He tried to sound positive, but truth was, he didn't know if they could.

"That's not the news I'm talking about," she said, moving out from behind the counter. "I wonder if you've ever heard the old saying, *Fool me once, shame on you, fool me twice, shame on me.*"

Vaughn frowned, not understanding. "What are you talking about?"

"You mentioned the name Natalie Nichols yesterday."

"Yes, she works for Value-X. She —"

"I met her this morning."

"Natalie's here?" Foolishly he'd assumed she'd spent the night in Grand Forks.

"She stayed at the 3 of a Kind last night. She's been trying to reach you — and here you are, right under her nose."

"I don't know what she told you, but —"

"She told me she was your fiancée."

It was all starting to make sense to Vaughn, a sick kind of sense. Natalie's declaration certainly explained that "shame me twice" stuff. "She spoke to your mother this morning," Carrie went on. "Your mother said if you weren't over at the bank to check here with Hassie. Only it was me she found."

"I can explain," he began.

"I'm sure you can, but frankly I'm not interested in listening." With that, she returned to the pharmaceutical counter and resumed her work as if he was no longer there.

Vaughn waited uncertainly for a moment, but she didn't look anywhere except at her task, at the pills she was counting out.

It was too late for explanations. Too late to regain her trust. Too late for him.

Chapter 10

Vaughn didn't think anything could happen to make this day any worse, but he was wrong.

As soon as he pulled into the driveway at his parents' home, he saw the unfamiliar car. Even before he'd climbed out of his own vehicle, he knew who'd come to visit.

Natalie.

Sure enough, the instant he walked into the house, his father cast him a sympathetic glance.

"You're back," his mother said, her voice strained and unnaturally high.

"Hello, Vaughn," Natalie said from the living room. She held a cup of coffee balanced on her knee. She looked out of place — and decidedly irritated.

He nodded in her direction.

"I think we'll leave the two of you to talk," his mother announced, and exited the room with the speed of someone who's relieved to escape. His father was directly behind her.

With a silent groan, Vaughn turned toward Natalie.

"You didn't answer my phone messages."

She set aside her coffee, glaring at him. "When I couldn't find you, I drove straight to Buffalo Valley, where I spent the night at some hole-in-the-wall. Merry Christmas, Natalie," she said bitterly.

She didn't appear to expect a comment, so he sat down across from her and waited. When she didn't immediately continue, he figured he'd better take his stand.

"I'm finished with Value-X." Nothing she could say or offer him would influence his decision. "You aren't going to change my mind."

"I'll say you're finished. I'll be fortunate to have a job myself after this."

Vaughn doubted that. Natalie was the type who'd always land on her feet. Yes, she'd recommended Vaughn to the company, but they couldn't hold that against her.

"You intend to go through with this . . . this craziness, don't you?"

No use hedging. "Yes, I do. I've resigned, and since I hadn't officially started work yet, I didn't bother to give any notice."

She sighed and stared down at her coffee. "I wonder if I ever knew you."

Vaughn said nothing. He'd let her say what she wanted, denounce him, threaten him, whatever. She had cause; he wasn't exactly blameless in all this.

"You think I don't know what this is about?" she challenged. She stood, crossing

211

her arms. "It all has to do with you and me."

Vaughn didn't know a kind way to tell her there *wasn't* any "you and me." There'd probably never been a "you and me." Not with Natalie. Looking at her, Vaughn wondered how he could ever have believed he was in love with her. The very traits that had once attracted him now repulsed him. Her ambition blinded her to everything that was unique and special about Buffalo Valley.

"Say something!" she shrilled.

"I'm sorry."

"That's a good start." Her stance relaxed somewhat.

"It doesn't change anything, though." He wasn't being purposely cruel, only frank. "I'm going to do everything I can to keep Value-X out of Buffalo Valley."

"You're mad at me," she insisted. "All this craziness about moving to some backwoods town is a form of punishment. You're trying to make me regret what I said. Vaughn, you simply don't understand how important Value-X is to me and to our future."

"Natalie —"

She ignored him and started pacing. "We've always been good together, Vaughn, you know that."

"Have we, Natalie?" he asked, hoping she was capable of admitting the truth.

"I can't let you do this," she said, clenching her fists.

He shook his head. "It's done."

"But you're destroying your career!"

"I don't want to work for a company like Value-X. Not now and not in the future."

"What are you going to do, then?"

"I don't know," he told her, and it was true. He'd fight the big retailer for as long as his money held out, but after that . . . he didn't have any answers.

"I can help you," she said. "You're this rough-and-ready Airborne Ranger, trying to be a hero. But you've got to face reality. No one goes against Value-X and walks away a winner. This will cost you more than you can afford to lose."

He ignored her threat. "Thanks but no thanks," he muttered.

She looked crestfallen.

Vaughn had a few questions of his own. "Why did you tell Carrie we're engaged?"

"Because we are!" she cried. "Did we or did we not discuss marriage?"

He didn't respond. She already had her answer.

"Oh, I get it," Natalie raged, her eyes spitting fire. "You found yourself a little side dish while you were away visiting Mom and Dad. You forgot all about me. Is *that* it?"

"We aren't engaged and we aren't getting married." She couldn't seriously believe he intended to continue this relationship when it was obviously a dead end for both of them.

"But we *did* discuss marriage on more than one occasion, and I never said I *wouldn't* marry you. We both understood we'd get married someday."

"I didn't see it that way. Yes, we talked about marriage, but there was no commitment — and very little interest on your part."

"Now you're lying, too."

He bristled, but bit his tongue before he said something he'd regret.

"Well . . . it's sort of a lie." Natalie lowered her head. "I made a mistake, but not once did I say anything about breaking off our relationship."

"It's over." He didn't know how much plainer he could be.

"I know." She sighed. "Well, if you insist on this lunacy, you're on your own."

He nodded.

"We could've been very good together," she whispered.

"I'm sorry."

"I know, and you'll be a whole lot sorrier once Value-X is through with this town." She rallied then, jerking her head up, chin tilted. "If you want to freeze your butt off in this horrible place, then go right ahead." She reached for her coat and yanked it toward her.

The sound of several car doors closing distracted Vaughn. He glanced out the window to see all four of Carrie's brothers standing in the driveway. He could only surmise that they'd come en masse to finish him off.

"Who's here?" Natalie asked.

"The firing squad," Vaughn answered.

"Terrific. Can I fire the first shot?"

Vaughn didn't respond to her sarcasm. He headed toward the front door, opening it for the four men who marched, single file, into the house. Soon Carrie's brothers stood in the middle of the room, looking from Vaughn to Natalie and then back.

"What happened?" Chuck demanded. "You left town without saying a word."

"I didn't meet with Heath," Vaughn started to explain, but wasn't given the opportunity before another question was hurled at him.

"Aren't you going to introduce us to your sister?"

"I'm Natalie Nichols." She introduced herself, stepping forward and offering each of the Hendrickson brothers her hand. "And I'm not Vaughn's sister."

"Then who are you?" Ken asked, frowning.

"His fiancée. Or I was," she said, "until recently, but now Vaughn's met someone else. He just told me that he no longer wishes to marry me." She appeared to be making a brave effort to hold her chin high and keep her lower lip from trembling. He'd never realized what a good actress Natalie was.

Vaughn resisted rolling his eyes. He remained silent, preferring not to get drawn into a theatrical scene in which *he* was identified as the villain.

"Someone will need to give me directions back to my hotel." She pulled a tissue from her pocket and dabbed at her eyes, being careful not to smear her mascara.

"I can get you there." Ken stepped forward. "I'll be happy to help."

Tom's gaze narrowed on Vaughn. "Did she have something to do with the fact that you didn't see Heath?"

Vaughn shook his head, surprised the Hendrickson brothers hadn't already heard. "The land sold."

"What the hell?"

All four brothers started speaking at once. As luck would have it, Vaughn's parents chose that precise moment to reappear.

"I thought I heard voices," his mother said as she came into the living room.

Tom motioned with his head toward Natalie. "You'd better have a good explanation," he muttered. "You'd better not be engaged to her and seeing Carrie."

"Yeah," Pete agreed. "This is all some kind of misunderstanding, isn't it? Didn't I tell you I'd make you pay if you hurt my sister?"

"He was never actually engaged," his mother said, hurrying to defend Vaughn. "What he told us is —"

That was when his father stepped into the

fray. "Barbara, let Vaughn answer for himself, would you?"

This was impossible. Everyone talked at once. Part of the conversation had to do with the land; everyone was clearly upset about that. Then Pete and his mother got involved in a debate about whether Vaughn should be dating Carrie. In the meantime, Ken and Natalie had apparently struck up a friendly conversation. They sat next to each other on the sofa, so close that their knees touched. Vaughn could only guess what she was saying, but frankly, he couldn't care less.

Before everything blew up in his face, Vaughn walked through the kitchen, grabbed his coat and stepped out the back door. He got into his car, which fortunately hadn't been blocked by the other vehicles. Glancing toward the house, he saw everyone gathered in front of the big window in the living room, staring at him. They must have been dumbfounded, because no one seemed to be speaking.

When he reached the end of the long driveway, Vaughn had to make a decision. He could go searching for solitude, a quiet place to recover his dignity. Or he could drive back to Buffalo Valley.

He chose Buffalo Valley. When he'd finished breaking Hassie's heart, he'd do what he could to mend Carrie's.

He'd never meant to hurt Carrie, but that

didn't discount the fact that he'd misled her. This wasn't exactly his finest hour.

When they'd first met, he'd found her charming. Later, when he got to know her, he'd been enchanted by her warmth, delighted by her love of family and home. Those were qualities that had come to mean a great deal to him. Carrie was *genuine*, and she was authentic in her relationships. Unlike him . . .

Vaughn wanted to kick himself for not being honest with her from the start. He didn't have a single excuse. All he could do now was pray that she'd be willing to accept him — and that she'd give him an opportunity to prove himself.

The hour's drive into town passed in a blur, and practically before he knew it he'd pulled off the highway and turned onto what were now familiar roads. Buffalo Valley stretched before him, but he viewed it with new eyes. He recalled his first visit, recalled how stark and bare the town had seemed, almost as if it were devoid of personality. He'd soon recognized how wrong he was.

While the buildings might be outdated and the lampposts antiques, the town itself represented the very heart of the country. The heart of America's heartland. It was where he wanted to be, how he wanted to live.

His mind was clear now. Easing the car into a parking space on Main Street, Vaughn forced himself to consider what he'd say to Hassie. It wasn't a task he relished.

All his talk of opening a feed store had done nothing but build up her hopes. Now he was about to disillusion an old woman who'd invested her whole life in a town that couldn't be saved. Whatever happened, though, he was staying in Buffalo Valley; he'd be part of its struggle and part of its future.

He dared not put this off any longer, and drawing a deep breath, he walked into the pharmacy.

The instant she saw him, Hassie cried out his name. "Vaughn, oh, Vaughn." Tears streaked her weathered cheeks as she hurried across the store, her arms stretched out toward him.

Apparently someone had already brought her the news. Holding open his own arms as she came to him, he hugged her, the sound of her sobs echoing in his ears.

"I'm so sorry," Vaughn whispered, wondering what he could say that would comfort her.

"Sorry?" Hassie eased back, gazing at him through watery eyes. "In the name of heaven, why would you be *sorry?* This is what we've hoped for all along."

Vaughn stared at her, not knowing what to think. "The land sold, Hassie."

"Yes, I know." She clapped her hands, eyes sparkling with delight. "This is better than anything I could've imagined."

"I'm . . . confused."

"I know." She patted his back and led him to the soda fountain. "Sit down," she ordered. "If there was ever a time for one of my chocolate sodas, this is it."

"What about Value-X?"

"They lost the land. The women of Buffalo Valley got to Ambrose before he signed the deal with Value-X and they bought it out from under the company. The ladies convinced Ambrose he'd be making a mistake."

Vaughn knew that several of the women in town owned businesses; he knew they had a big stake in the community. It floored him that they'd managed to do what no one else had deemed possible.

"But how . . . when?"

"Do you recall when the women got together?" Hassie asked, leaning over the refrigeration unit, scooping up the ice cream.

"I remember a cookie exchange." Carrie had mentioned something along those lines earlier in the week.

"The meeting took place after that," Hassie said. "Then a committee of six paid Ambrose a visit. I don't know everything they said, but apparently they convinced him to sell *them* those twenty acres. I hear they twisted his arm by appealing to his vanity — promising to name the school after him. He liked that. He also liked the fact that he could sell his land at the same price Value-X offered."

"Is Value-X seeking out any other property?"

Hassie grinned. "They can try, but there isn't a single person in this area who'd sell to them — not at any price."

Vaughn nodded, still feeling a little numb. "What do the women intend to do with the property?" he asked.

Hassie's grin widened. "You mean you don't know?"

He didn't. Since they were all capable, business-minded individuals, Vaughn suspected they already had plans.

Hassie chuckled softly. "You'll have to ask them, but my guess is they'd be willing to sell you a portion of it — that is, if you're still inclined to settle in Buffalo Valley."

Vaughn could barely take it in. "You mean that?"

"Talk to Sarah Urlacher and she'll give you all the details."

"I need to see Carrie first."

Hassie set the glass on the counter. "Ah, yes, Carrie." She made a tsking sound and plunked a paper straw into the thick chocolate soda. "You've got your work cut out there."

Vaughn wrapped his hand around the glass, feeling the cold against his palm. "I assume she's upset."

"That's one way of putting it."

Vaughn slid off the stool. He didn't want to offend Hassie by not drinking the soda, but he'd feel worlds better once he resolved the situation with Carrie. "She at home?"

"Doubt it." Hassie reached for the soda herself and took a long sip before she continued. "My guess is she's sitting on the swings over in the park. I found she likes to go there when something's troubling her. Look there first and if you can't find her, then check the house."

Vaughn thanked her and left immediately. He jogged across the street to the park. The snow forts he'd helped build on Christmas Day — was that only yesterday? — were still standing, a little the worse for wear. Following the freshly shoveled walk, Vaughn made his way toward the play equipment.

Hassie had, as always, given him the right advice. Carrie sat in the middle swing. Her face was red from the cold, and he wondered how long she'd been there.

Vaughn ached to tell her how sorry he was, but he feared that if he said or did the wrong thing now, he might lose her forever.

As he approached, Carrie glanced up, but she didn't acknowledge him. Vaughn, needing to gather his thoughts, didn't say anything, either. Instead, he settled into the swing beside her and waited for the words to come.

"I hurt you, didn't I?" he asked after an awkward moment.

"Were you engaged to her when you came to town?"

This was the difficult part. "No. No, I wasn't."

"She seemed to think so."

He gripped the chain and shifted sideways to see Carrie more clearly. "Before I left Seattle, Natalie and I talked about marriage."

The words seemed to hit her hard.

"She wasn't interested."

"Apparently she's changed her mind."

Vaughn saw that Carrie was staring straight ahead, as though mesmerized by whatever she was watching. "So have I."

Carrie turned toward him, but when their eyes met, she turned away again. "Why?"

"I met someone else."

"You must be a very fickle man, Vaughn Kyle, to ask one woman to marry you and then, while she's making up her mind, start seeing another."

"I realize how bad it sounds."

"Sounds, nothing! Underhanded and unfair is more like it."

"You're right," he said simply. "I have no excuse."

"You must've really enjoyed hearing me spill out my heart." She covered her cheeks with both hands and closed her eyes, as if remembering the things she'd said. They seemed to embarrass her now.

"Carrie, no! It wasn't like that." He thought

about the afternoon she'd told him about her ex-husband. He didn't know how to put into words what her trust had done for him. How her straightforward devotion had wiped out the cynicism he'd felt after Natalie's opportunistic approach to love and marriage.

"You're certainly not the kind of man I'd want in my life."

"I need you, Carrie. . . ."

"For what, comic relief?"

"We've only known each other a short while. Who can say where this relationship will take us? Maybe you're right. After you get to know me better, you could very well decide you don't want any more to do with me. If that's the case, I'll accept it. All I'm asking for is a chance."

"To break my heart?"

"No, to give you mine."

She didn't answer him for the longest time. Finally her mouth twisted wryly and she said, "You're afraid of what my brothers will do to you once they learn about . . . Natalie, aren't you?"

"No man in his right mind would voluntarily tangle with your brothers," he replied, deciding this was not the moment to tell her they'd already met the woman in question. "However, I figure I can take them on if it comes to that. What I'm telling you now has nothing to do with your brothers. It's how I feel about you."

"Don't!" she cried with such passion that Vaughn jumped. "Don't say things you don't mean."

"I am completely sincere." He slid off the swing and crouched down in front of her. He wanted her to see how vulnerable he was to her. Taking her right hand in his, he removed her glove and kissed the inside of her palm.

She pulled back her hand.

"I plan to stay in Buffalo Valley," he continued, undaunted.

Her eyes widened, but she bit her lower lip as if to suppress her reaction.

"I'm going to invest in the community, become part of it, make a contribution."

Carrie's gaze darted away and then returned. "Don't tell me things like that just because you think it's what I want to hear."

"It's true, Carrie."

She closed her eyes and lowered her chin. "I want so badly to believe you."

"Believe me," he whispered, then nuzzled her throat. He didn't kiss her, although the temptation was strong. "All I'm asking for is another chance," he said again.

"Oh, Vaughn." She pressed her hands against his shoulders — to bring him closer or push him away?

Vaughn helped make the decision for her. Crouched down as he was, his face level with her own, he leaned toward her and grazed her lips with his. Her mouth was cold, yet moist and welcoming. She moaned softly and he rubbed his warm lips over hers, seducing her into deepening the kiss.

One moment he was crouched in front of Carrie and she was leaning forward, giving herself to the kiss. The next he was losing his balance and tumbling backward.

Carrie let out a small cry of alarm as she went with him. Vaughn did what he could to protect her. He threw his arms around her waist and took the brunt of the impact as she landed on top of him in the snow.

"You've knocked me off balance from the moment we met," he said.

Carrie smiled then, for the first time since he'd joined her. "You've done the same thing to me."

"Good."

"No promises, Vaughn."

"I disagree." He brushed the hair from her face, barely aware of the snow and the cold.

She frowned. "What do you mean?"

"There's promise every time I look at you, Carrie Hendrickson. Promise each time I kiss you." Then, because he couldn't keep himself from doing so, he showed her exactly what he meant.

As soon as their lips met, Carrie whimpered and he wrapped his arms more firmly around her.

"This is only the beginning for us," he whispered.

Carrie placed her head on his shoulder and gave a shuddering sigh.

"I was never really worried about your brothers," Vaughn confessed. "*You* were always the one who terrified me." He laughed and rolled, reversing their positions in the snow. Her eyes were smiling as he gazed down on her.

"So you want to give me your heart?" she said, looking up at him. She flattened her hand against his coat.

"Don't you know?" he asked her.

"Know what?"

"You already have it." And then he went about proving it.

Mr. and Mrs. William Hendrickson
and
Mr. and Mrs. Richard Kyle
Request the honor of your presence at a reception to
celebrate
the marriage of their children
Carrie Ann Hendrickson
and
Vaughn Richard Kyle
When: December 15th
Where: Buffalo Bob's 3 of a Kind
Main Street,
Buffalo Valley, North Dakota
RSVP

About the Author

New York Times bestselling author **Debbie Macomber** brings readers back to the fictional town of Buffalo Valley, North Dakota. She is a multi-award-winning writer with more than 60 million copies of her books in print, including *Dakota Born*, *Dakota Home* and *Always Dakota*, her previous stories about the people of Buffalo Valley.

Debbie Macomber lives in the state of Washington with her husband, Wayne, but her family, on both sides, is from the Dakotas.

We hope you have enjoyed this Large Print book. Other Thorndike, Wheeler or Chivers Press Large Print books are available at your library or directly from the publishers.

For more information about current and upcoming titles, please call or write, without obligation, to:

Publisher
Thorndike Press
295 Kennedy Memorial Drive
Waterville, ME   04901
Tel. (800) 223-1244

Or visit our Web site at:
www.gale.com/thorndike
www.gale.com/wheeler

OR

Chivers Large Print
published by BBC Audiobooks Ltd
St James House, The Square
Lower Bristol Road
Bath BA2 3SB
England
Tel.   +44(0) 800 136919
email: bbcaudiobooks@bbc.co.uk
www.bbcaudiobooks.co.uk

All our Large Print titles are designed for easy reading, and all our books are made to last.